CLAIRE AND THE GOSPEL BUS BOOK 9

Claire Here There and Everywhere

Lin Joy

Copyright © 2023 Lin Joy

All rights reserved

The characters and events portrayed in this book are fictitious. Any similarity to real persons, living or dead, is coincidental and not intended by the author.

No part of this book may be reproduced, or stored in a retrieval system, or transmitted in any form or by any means, electronic, mechanical, photocopying, recording, or otherwise, without express written permission of the publisher.

CHAPTER 1

Claire to the Rescue

The morning sun found Claire in her bedroom ready to go out into the back garden and welcome her rabbit Hoppity Hop, and her two hens, Big Bird and Wee Gem to their new day. She had been reading all night sitting on her chair while at the same time being charged up. She left the servants' quarters and entered the kitchen where her mother, who was the housekeeper, Mrs Low the cook and Bella the maid were getting ready to start their day's work. After wishing them all a good morning she then called on her two dogs, Big Dog and Mitzy to follow her out into the garden.

After feeding and watering her pet hens, Big Bird and Wee Gem, then her rabbit Hoppity Hop, she returned to the kitchen to help with the work. The staff then had their own early breakfast and then prepared Mr and Mrs Goodyard's breakfast, who got up not quite as early as the staff. Claire, when her work was finished, would take her dogs for an early morning walk over the fields and along country roads.

There was a field next to a road on Claire's walk, where there was an old horse called Lucky. The owner of Lucky, a certain Mr Radcliffe, had recently bought the farm which included the field where Lucky was kept. When the farm was bought, Lucky, came with the farm which had annoyed Mr Radcliffe, who now felt he was lumbered with Lucky, so he just left Lucky in the field day and night and got a farm worker to make sure it was fed and watered. His daughter was a qualified riding instructor, so he had emptied Lucky's stable to make way for her horses from her riding school, which she had closed down when she moved into one of the farm buildings.

Now every day when Claire was walking the dogs, she would bring Lucky a carrot. Claire began to notice that Lucky's appearance seemed to deteriorate day by day, so she was determined to act to save Lucky. One day an opportunity arose to save Lucky, so Claire acted.

CHAPTER 2
The Children to the Rescue

Whenever she could, Claire was to be found at *Vets,Vets, Vets,* the charity that helps sick animals. It was there on the following Saturday morning she overheard two of the young volunteer vets talking about Mr Radcliffe, the reluctant owner of Lucky. It appeared that Mr Radcliffe was having a clear out at his new farm, and that included getting rid of Lucky, who had always stayed there. Not even the families of the gangsters that had inhabited the farm before Mr Radcliffe, got rid of Lucky. It is a strange fact that many bad people are much kinder to their pets than people would expect.

"That Radcliffe chap actually had the audacity to phone the surgery to ask if I knew of a suitable knacker man who would take Lucky to a glue factory and sell the horse for him. I gave him short shift, I can assure you," said Dr. Lambert, the older of the two young vets, who Claire knew to speak to.

"Quite right," said the other vet. "I would have done the same."

As soon as Claire's morning tasks were finished,

she headed for Rosie's farmhouse which was close to Lucky's field. Rosie was feeding the hens when Claire burst in on her. She was upset on hearing the news, but she was not surprised. "I have seen the way he treats his other animals too, and it is disgusting," said Rosie, who was now rather annoyed. "Something must be done about it." They then phoned Eleanor who was equally disgusted by Mr Radcliffe's words. Before they went on their way Claire asked each of them if they could meet again outside her house at three pm as she might have some good news. They suggested that Claire bring Jennifer along too, which pleased Claire greatly, for she was going to suggest the very same thing.

They did meet and plans were laid to rescue Lucky as soon as possible. They also told Claire all they knew about Mr Radcliffe. Claire learned that he used to own a pet store in the village for the usual dogs and cat food, but it also sold supplies for horses and poultry. When he had bought the farm he sold the shop in the village and opened a shop at his farm which saved him quite a bit of money.

Claire did not go straight home, but called in to see Jennifer and tell her about Lucky going to the knacker's yard. She was outraged and wanted to help save him. The first thing Claire and Jennifer did was to go and visit Mrs Flowers and tell her about Lucky. "What we need," explained Claire, "is a stable where we can hide Lucky, probably for the rest of his life, or until Mr Radcliffe forgets all about his horse. If he is sending it to the knackers yard then he must not really care about him, and hopefully will soon forget what he looked like. So we were wondering, Mrs Flowers, if...."

"If I could let you use my stable. Is that what you were going to ask, Claire?" Claire had been looking at Mrs Flowers with her large, pleading eyes which Mrs Flowers knew only too well.

"Yes it is," answered Claire. Mrs Flowers gave her consent. Claire's plan had worked out perfectly. At three pm Claire and Jennifer met Rosie and Eleanor outside Claire's house and off they went to see the stable. That afternoon the four children got the stable ready for Lucky. Eleanor and Rosie said they would supply the fresh straw and food from their farms the next day, so when the day came that Lucky was rescued everything would be ready for him.

CHAPTER 3

Claire to the Rescue

That very Saturday night, when darkness fell, Claire, dressed in her crow outfit, left her room through her bedroom window and headed for the paddock where Lucky was kept. The paddock was fenced off from the surrounding fields and the road that ran along the side of the paddock. There was a padlocked gate from the road into the paddock which was the only exit and entrance from the road, but there was another padlocked gate that gave entrance to the paddock from the surrounding fields. The success of the mission depended on Claire's ability to open that very padlock. She used her string of skeleton keys one after another, but to no avail until she had only a few left to try. She could just pull the gate off from its hinges and enter, but that would give the game away, for it would let everyone know that the horse thief entered via the fields and left the same way with Lucky. Claire said an emergency prayer and to her relief the next key she used opened the padlock, letting her walk in.

Claire went straight to the other end of the paddock which was next to the road. She had brought an iron bar with her and using her great strength and the iron bar, she ripped the padlock from off that gate. She then opened her backpack and brought out a small bottle of tractor oil which she placed several drops on the road to give the impression that a lorry had been parked there. It was a very quiet and lonely road and as she worked no vehicles passed by.

She then went and collected Lucky and placed a thick rope round his neck and then led him out of the paddock, through the gate into the field. Finally she locked the gate leaving it as she had found it and headed to the awaiting stable. Soon Lucky was safe and sound in Mrs Flowers' stable and Claire was back in her room.

When Sunday morning arrived, Jennifer as soon as she got out of bed, went to the stable, for she was sure she had heard the sounds of a horse neighing, and wanted to reassure herself that she was not just imagining things. When she got to the stable door she looked in and gave a cry of surprise, for there stood Claire, carrot in hand feeding Lucky. When Eleanor and Rosie arrived they were taken to the stable by Claire and Jennifer. The stable door was opened and they all looked in to see Lucky wondering who these strangers were. They all went up to Lucky and made a great fuss over him. It was then someone entered the stable. The children turned round and found a smiling Mrs Flowers.

CHAPTER 4
Dr Lambert and Lucky

"You have rescued Lucky!" said an amazed Mrs Flowers. "Well done, the four of you. You have certainly made this old stable fit for such a nice horse as Lucky. Now you must let me know if you need anything in the way of food or medicine for Lucky."

"Thank you," said Eleanor. "Rosie and I are just off to collect some food and straw from our farms and I will ask my dad to bring it here in his car. We don't want any vans or tractors calling here that would give the game away."

"And be assured," said Mrs Flowers, "I shan't be buying any horse stuff from that Ratcliffe pet shop, or any shop near here. I shall see you all later in church, and remember Mum's the word."

It was the following Saturday when the story of Lucky appeared in the local weekly newspaper. Claire had been working at the vets that morning and was in the staff room helping serve cups of tea and coffee, when in walked Dr Lambert for his morning break. He picked up the local paper then sat down in his usual seat to read it, and drank his usual cup of tea which Claire had placed next to him. He had almost finished drinking his tea, while reading the newspaper, when he suddenly jumped to his feet. "I have never read such rubbish in all my life," he cried, as he gazed at the article about Lucky in the local paper. "I just can't believe the hypocrisy of this man!" he exclaimed. "This Mr Radcliffe is the very man who wanted to sell Lucky to the knacker's yard and is now spewing out his lies, saying that he was terribly upset, believing that the horse would either land up in a glue factory or as pet food somewhere or other. I have heard of virtue signalling, but doesn't this beat all?" He threw down the newspaper onto the coffee table. "Next time I see him I shall give him a piece of my mind." He strode to and fro in the room lambasting Mr Ratcliffe for the lies he had been telling while the others in the room looked on.

Claire thought it was time to intervene, so she waited for the moment when he was heading towards her. "Would you like another cup of tea, Dr Lambert," asked Claire.

"Oh yes, Claire. That's just what I need," he answered, as he sat back down and sighed.

When the morning break was over and the staff were leaving the common room, Claire again approached Dr Lambert. "Did you enjoy your tea?"

"Yes I did, Claire, thank you. It calmed me down. I don't want to be shaking with rage when I now have a delicate operation on Tibby to perform. The others in the room had now left so Claire walked to the door with Dr Lambert.

"I wouldn't worry about Lucky, Dr Lambert. I'm sure he is safe right now and in the care of those who love horses," said Claire, with such conviction that Dr Lambert believed every word Claire had just spoken. He was not going to say something clumsy and interrogate her. He just gazed down at Claire, never said a word and smiled. He had known Claire now for quite a while and all the good works she had done for the charity. Claire smiled back. "Well," she said, "I now have to clean up all these cups and saucers.

Claire," he said, as he held out his hand for her inspection, "I'm not shaking any more."

CHAPTER 5

Lucky's New Home

Every day Claire and Jennifer would clean out Lucky's stable and take him out into the yard for exercise, as it was very important that Lucky's joints did not get stiff or stock up. They would make sure that he was given fresh water and was properly fed. What worried them greatly was the question of exercise for Lucky. Mrs Flowers owned the small paddock next to her mansion, but that was visible from the roadway. It would have been an ideal place to exercise Lucky, had it not been that Lucky was a well known, loved horse, and word would soon spread around the area that Lucky was back. Of course, the Radcliffe family would also probably hear about Lucky.

One day, after returning from school, and just having finished cleaning out the stable, Claire and Jennifer decided to tell Mrs Flowers of their anxiety. "Now that is a problem," said Mrs Flowers, after hearing their concern for Lucky. She thought for a moment then spoke. "I have a friend who runs a small animal sanctuary and I'm sure she would look after Lucky if I asked her. In fact, I shall phone her right now." Her friend, Miss Heywood, was delighted to help and told Mrs Flowers she could accommodate Lucky at any time, but to let her know when they decided Lucky would be arriving.

"I know a vet, Dr Lambert, from the charity *Vets Vets Vets* who is a big fan of Lucky," said Claire. "He gave me his card and told me that if I needed any help just call. He won't give us away. He will never tell anyone that Lucky is here. May I bring him to see Lucky the next time he is at the vet's charity, Mrs Flowers?"

"Certainly, he sounds like an honest person who would not betray our secret." Well, on Saturday at the vets Claire asked him to call in at Mrs Flowers' after his shift. He did call and was met by Claire on Mrs Flowers driveway. Claire then escorted him to the stable.

"You are not going to tell me Claire, that you keep a horse too?" laughed Dr Lambert, when he saw the stable. Claire introduced him to Mrs Flowers and Jennifer, after which they all entered the stable.

"It's Lucky!" exclaimed Dr Lambert, and went straight over and gave Lucky a neck hug. "Well, I must say you all have done well. You all have saved Lucky from being turned into pots of glue scattered all over this country. I don't want to know how you rescued Lucky, but I am so glad you did." Dr Lambert examined Lucky, while the rest of them waited outside for his prognosis. When he emerged from the stable he looked quite worried. "Lucky is in need of lots of exercises, so we need to get him into a field and give him a run around." Mrs Flowers told the vet about what they had planned and he was well pleased. "When are you planning to transport Lucky to his new home?" asked Dr Lambert.

"When my helpers will not be at school," replied Mrs Flowers.

"Well I shall come here next Saturday morning towing a horse trailer and help hook it up to your car and I shall help you place Lucky in it, if that meets your approval?"

"Yes, it does and is very kind of you, but where are you going to get a horse trailer from?"

"We have one that we keep in the garage at our Veterinary Practice. My father, whose practice it is, acquired the horse trailer years ago. Once you are finished with it you can return it to the practice."

"How much will I need to bring to rent it for a day?" asked Mrs Flowers.

"Not a penny," replied Dr Lambert, who hurried off to his car before Mrs Flowers could say another word. To him, Mrs Flowers and the children were heroes having rescued Lucky. He had become a vet to help animals and he had no intention of taking a penny from his group of heroes.

The next Saturday morning found Claire and her friends Jennifer, Eleanor and Rosie along with Mrs Flowers at Lucky's stable awaiting the arrival of Dr Lambert and the horse trailer. He did not disappoint and arrived at the arranged time. He got out of his car, unhooked the trailer and attached it to Mrs Flowser's car. It wasn't easy that morning getting Lucky into the horse trailer, but they managed.

Dr Lambert locked the back door of the trailer and handed Claire the key. "You are in charge of the trailer, Claire," he said. "When you bring back the trailer just hand in the key to the receptionist. Good luck everyone, you are all doing a noble work." They all thanked him for his help. "I shall have to leave now and get to work," and so saying he got into his car and drove off.

If truth be told, Lucky had been stolen and they would be taking a stolen horse to a better place of safety. Claire had dug out some fake licence plates she had and put them onto the car and horse trailer. Soon Mrs Flowers and the children, with Lucky in the trailer, were on the road heading towards Lucky's new home, while Dr Lambert was heading to the veterinary Charity.

CHAPTER 6

The Incident in the Car Park

After driving for some time Mrs Flowers pulled into a fast-food restaurant and parked in a quiet corner of the car park. "I'll stay and look after Lucky," said Claire, для I have had breakfast, but I know some of you had to go without."

"I'll stay with Claire," said Jennifer, "for I have eaten too."

"May I suggest you leave the car keys with me Mr Flowers," suggested Claire. "Just in case." Mrs Flowers for some reason or another handed the keys to Claire and then set off with Eleanor and Rosie to the fast-food restaurant, leaving Claire and Jennifer guarding the horse trailer and car.

It was just a few minutes later that a group of youths approached Claire and Jennifer. They were dressed to scare, but to Claire they just looked like a group of rather silly looking boys.

"What have you got in there?" asked their leader, pointing at the horse trailer.

"A horse," answered Claire, not at all cowered by his appearance. "Would you like to look in at the back of the trailer?" He said nothing, but went to the back of the trailer where Claire opened the top part of the door, so he could look in.

"I just see its tail and back," he said, as he gripped the handle and tried to open the door, but failed. "Open this door," he yelled, as his face was starting to turn red with rage.

"I have no intention of opening the door," said Claire ever so calmly, causing his face to grow even redder.

"If you don't open it and bring out the horse to let my friends see it, then we'll topple your stupid wooden trailer on its side and smash it to bits so the horse can get out and run about."

"He wants the horse free so it can run about the car park causing havoc," said Claire to herself, "but not if I can help it." Claire noticed that his followers were slowly approaching the trailer while looking towards their leader waiting for him to give the signal to start. Jennifer, who was standing next to Claire, was showing signs of anxiety. "Wait," Claire called out. "I'll find the key. You stay here Glenda and look after the horse." No, Claire did not get Jennifer's name mixed up, it was deliberate. Jennifer understood. Claire went to the car and opened the driver's door, but did not enter. "Glenda, come and help me find the key to the trailer," shouted Claire.

"OK Sue," called Jennifer, and joined Claire at the side of the car. Claire entered the car where she sat down in the driver's seat and made out as if she was searching for the key. Jennifer noticed Claire had one hand on the ignition key, so she went into the car and sat down in the passenger seat.

"Close the door Jennifer, the moment I start the engine," whispered Claire.

"Hurry up you two and find that key," shouted the gang leader.

"I have got the key now," shouted Claire, who at that very moment turned on the ignition. The car doors were closed and the car along with the trailer moved off. Mrs Flowers' car was in fact a powerful four by four and easily accelerated away from the gang before they had realised what had happened. Not for a moment did they think that a girl like Claire could drive a car, never mind one towing a horse trailer. When they realised what had happened they started running after Claire, but it was too late for Claire had now parked in a busy part of the car park, where there would be lots of people with smartphones ready to record any incident that happened.

However, the gang did not leave, but sat in their truck watching Claire, ready to follow her when she left. "Jennifer, I want you to go into the restaurant and tell Mrs Flowers what has happened, and tell her when she leaves not to go back to her car, but to go with the girls to the car park exit where no one shall see them. I shall pick them up when I leave," said Claire, as she went into her backpack and brought out two spiked objects. "I want you to give one to Rosie and one to Eleanor to place under the wheels of the gang's truck. At the back of the gang's truck there is a wall and pavement so they will be moving forward. Eleanor and Rosie can walk along the pavement then place the spikes. It is dangerous so tell them not to take any chances. I'll do my best to distract the gang. After you see Mrs Flowers you have to come back here, Jennifer."

So Jennifer left and gave Mrs Flowers the message, and to Eleanor and Rosie she gave each a pointed steel tyre buster to place under the gang's truck, which she pointed out through the windows of the restaurant. Jennifer was soon back in the car sitting next to Claire while they waited for Mrs Flowers and the two girls to appear from the restaurant.

They soon left the restaurant and made their way along the pavement next to the wall, just as Jennifer had instructed them to do. Claire now got out of Mrs Flowers' four by four and walked towards the gang's truck, so when Rosie and Eleanor were about to reach the truck, Claire just happened to trip over a speed bump and fall flat on her face. At that very moment the two tyre busters were placed under the truck. Claire hobbled back to the car and winked at Jennifer.

Five minutes later Claire started the car and headed for the exit. The gang started their truck and moved forward, but they went nowhere, for they had two flat back tyres. Claire then drove out of the car park, and there just around the corner, waiting for them, were her three friends. They again were soon heading for Lucky's new home with Mrs Flowers at the wheel.

When they arrived at their destination they were greeted by Mrs Flowers' friend, Miss Heywood. She showed them where Lucky would be stabled and the field where he would be free to run around. Claire removed the fake registration plates on the car and horse trailer and they all thanked Miss Heywood for her help. Soon they were on their way home using a different route from the one that brought them there. Their first stop was the vets where they unhooked the horse trailer and left it behind the car park. With all that done, Claire handed in the trailer key to the receptionist. Mrs Flowers drove them to her house where they all thanked God for watching over them and then had a very nice lunch.

CHAPTER 7
The New Girl

There was a new girl called Betsy in Claire's maths class and it did not take long to find out that she was anything but a nice person. Betsy was a bully, and for the first week at her new school Betsy looked around for someone to bully. The first person whose life she made miserable by bullying was that of Muriel, a timid girl, well behaved and a hard worker. One thing Betsy hated most of all was a well behaved pupil and that was probably the main reason she chose Muriel to bully.

One day at the start of the lunch break, Claire was chatting to Muriel heading for the canteen, when along came Betsy and deliberately bumped into Muriel as she walked by. Betsy stopped immediately and turned and looked straight at Muriel. "Watch who you bump into you sour-faced brat," yelled Betsy. "You better apologise or else."

Muriel was completely lost for words, but not Claire. "It was you who bumped into my friend and you did it deliberately. If anyone is to apologise it surely is you. You just run along and leave us alone."

Now it was Betsy who was lost for words, but just for a moment. She never expected anyone to stand up to her as Claire had just done. She prided herself in her appearance on being a rather nasty, hard as nails and vindictive looking person. She now was angry, very angry.

"Shut up, brat," she yelled at Claire, and then she lost it. She aimed a punch straight at Claire's face, but missed and just could not believe how that happened. She got ready to throw another punch, so she drew herself up to her greatest height and then thrust her whole body at Claire at the same time throwing her punch. The punch was meant to land on Claire's face and Claire's body was meant to be knocked to the ground. It was an easy punch for Claire to avoid, for she saw it coming even before Betsy threw it. Claire had met many bullies in her school life and Betsy was one of the most inapt she had come across. It had ended with Betsy lying flat, face down on the ground. Claire went up to her and looked down.

"May I give you a hand up?" she asked very politely. This seemed to infuriate Betsy, who started beating her fists on the ground.

"I'm going to report you for this," she yelled. "You are in big trouble."

There had been quite a number of onlookers to the incident and some burst out laughing at her ridiculous allegations. The scorn seemed to revive Betsy and she jumped to her feet. She looked around and swore at them all, and then with head held high off she marched down the corridor. She never did report Claire.

"Thank you for standing up for me, Claire," said Muriel. Claire looked at Muriel and smiled as a recognition of her thanks.

"You won't need to worry about Betsy trying to bully you any more," said Claire. "She will have forgotten about you. Did you see her face full of hatred for me? She has just made a fool of herself and she will blame me for it. She is always going to hate me, but I don't think she will tangle with me again. Bullies are cowards. Let's go to the canteen. Would you like to join me and my friends at our table?"

"Why, yes! Very much indeed, Claire. Thank you," answered Muriel.

CHAPTER 8

The Missing Parrot

One day, Mrs Flowers asked Claire to come over to see her after school. They met in Mrs Flowers' sitting room where Mrs Flowers asked Claire if she could get Molly to come and help find a missing parrot. The parrot belonged to a elderly lady, Miss Clifton, a friend of Mrs Flowers, who lived on her own in a neighbouring village. "She has had this parrot for twenty eight years and now it has been stolen from her home," explained Mrs Flowers. "She is very upset and we were wondering if you could ask Molly to find the parrot for her, Claire?"

Claire phoned Molly only to find she was busy on another case altogether. "You don't mind then if I take on the case, Molly?" asked Claire.

"No, not at all, and I hope you succeed in solving it," answered Molly. Mrs Flowers was not too keen on Claire taking the case, as it could be dangerous, but Claire persuaded her otherwise. Now it was Claire's case. Mrs Flowers also showed Claire some photos she had of Miss Clifton, her parrot and her house. That night Claire went on the internet and studied a selection of maps of the region around Miss Clifton's house and further afield. She also read about what went on in the districts so by the morning she probably knew just as much as those who stayed there. She had found that at the foot of Miss Clifton's garden was a river, and several miles down the river was a branch of a large home entertainment company which produced movies and TV programmes.

Next day was Friday, so after school Mrs Flowers took Claire and Jennifer to see Miss Clifton. Claire was shocked when she saw the old lady having previously seen a recent photograph of her. Losing her parrot had made her look much older than she actually was. Mrs Flowers explained to Miss Clifton that Claire had come to try and retrieve the parrot. "I don't think a little girl like her will be able to find Percy," said Miss Clifton, when she thought Claire was out of hearing distance. Mrs Flowers, thinking that Claire may have heard, glanced over at Claire. Claire caught her look but simply shrugged her shoulders and spread her hands to show the remark did not bother her at all.

Claire then went into the garden alone to look around. The garden ran all the way down to the river where there was a small boathouse. Claire looked in through the window and noticed a rowing boat with a set of oars. On seeing it she smiled as she now had a plan.

When Claire returned to the house she was the

first to speak. "If I'm going to solve this case I will need to stay here from this Saturday afternoon till Sunday morning. I will also require the use of your rowing boat for a short period of time," she told Miss Clifton. Miss Clifton just did not know what to say, so Mrs Flowers came to her rescue.

"Both Jennifer and I will also be staying to keep you company," said |Mrs Flowers.

"Very well," said Miss Clifton, after thinking it over. She then turned and looked Claire straight in the eye. "If you have not found my Percy by Sunday afternoon then I must ask you all to leave, and then I shall go about finding a proper detective to find my Percy." Mrs Flowers gasped at her friend's very rude behaviour. She looked over at Claire to see what effect it had on her. Claire just smiled and winked.

It seemed Claire had annoyed Miss Clifton in some way, and Claire had a good idea why that was. "Tell me Miss Clifton, what did you do before you retired?"

"I was the headteacher at a girl's school. Is that relevant? Surely you are not suggesting that one of my former pupils did this as revenge for something I did? What utter nonsense!"

Claire simply shrugged her shoulders and said nothing. "So she was a headteacher, I thought so," said Claire to herself. "She doesn't not like me in her house and she sure does not like me suggesting that I would like to stay here on Saturday night."

"If your parrot is not back in your house by Sunday morning, I shall leave immediately," said Claire, with confidence in her voice. "Meantime, if you could please gather together as many recent photos you have of your parrot and the cage it was in, that would be most helpful. Well thank you for all your help Miss Clifton and don't worry, for I hope to have your parrot back home here by Sunday morning. Now if Mrs Flowers and Jennifer are agreeable, I think it's best we head back home".

They did leave after Mrs Flowers had a few calming words with her friend .In the journey home Mrs Flowers apologised for her friends behaviour. "It was just water off a duck's back," said Claire. "She used to be a school teacher and she is still not used to children like me asking favours from her. It does not bother me if she is slightly abrupt."

CHAPTER 9

The Rescue

Claire's mum consented to Claire having a sleep over at Miss Clifton's house by the river. After diner on Saturday evening, Mrs Flowers, along with Jennifer, came and collected Claire. When they arrived at Miss Clifton's house, Claire and Jennifer were shown to their room at the back of the house. When bedtime came Claire told Jennifer that she would be spending the night outside the house. When darkness was fast setting in, Claire put on her black crow outfit and left the house via their bedroom window and stepped into the dark, black, moonless night. She hoped to return and be back with Jennifer before dawn, and would tap at the window to be let back in.

Just a short time later found Claire in Miss Clifton's rowing boat, rowing down the river heading to her destination, the destination being none other than the studios of the home entertainment company. She had done her homework and found that they were making a series of movies featuring pirates, the star of the series being Long John Silver. "Now everybody knows where Captain Silver is to be found, there is bound to be a parrot," said Claire to herself. "The parrot they had been using must have died suddenly and someone probably knew where to find a lookalike replacement quickly, namely at Miss Clifton's house."

She soon arrived opposite the movie studios and left the rowing boat tied up among the reeds growing at the side of the river. From there she had a good view of the back of the studio's huts and smaller buildings that were scattered here and there along the river bank. Claire was interested in the huts for she was sure that the animals and birds used in their movies must be housed there. By careful listening and looking she soon found the hut where the birds were kept. Using her skeleton keys she got into the hut, and found what looked like a cage covered with a cloth. She removed the cloth and there was Percy the parrot sitting on his perch in the very cage that it had been in Miss Clifton's sitting room photos. Claire examined the parrot, and found it was indeed Percy. She covered up the cage and then left with Percy in his cage, locking the door behind her. All had gone well and now all that was left to do was to get back to the boat and row away up the river, but things did not quite work out as planned.

Claire was halfway to the boat when Percy found his voice. To Claire's astonishment Percy began to swear, repeating the same swear word over and over again. Claire now ran even faster than before. Percy's voice broke the silence of the night for the sound Percy made was loud and aggressive like that from a very annoyed individual. Suddenly the place was flooded with light and the security alarm sounded. A voice on a loudspeaker rang out. "Stop or I shall set the dogs on you." Claire just kept on going, getting nearer and nearer to the boat, but carrying the cage was slowing her down. Nevertheless, she managed to get into the boat safely with Percy, untied the boat and pushed it away from the river bank just in time before the dogs showed up barking and snarling.

In the distance was their handler looking rather out of shape, but doing his best to catch up with his dogs. Fortunately for Claire he was rather slow, so by the time he arrived Claire was well out of sight as she kept close to the river bank on her journey up the river. Percy by this time now had stopped squawking which made Claire look at him and shake her head. "You just could not keep quiet, could you when it mattered? Have you any idea what could have happened to both of us if the dogs had caught up on us, Percy? They would have had you, Percy the Parrot, for breakfast." Claire then thanked God for their deliverance and kept on rowing.

CHAPTER 10

The Surprise

Imagine the surprise on Jennifer's face when Claire tapped on the bedroom window and handed her the cage. "What's in the cage?" asked Jennifer.

"Remove the cover and see," suggested Claire.

"Oh, it's a parrot. Where did you buy it at this time of night?"

"Wait for the dawn, then all will be revealed. The important thing right now is that you get back to bed and get some well earned sleep."

At breakfast, while they all sat around the kitchen table, Miss Clifton was to ask the question she had been wanting to find the answer to since she went to bed last night. "You'll be leaving as soon as you finish breakfast I presume, Claire?"

"Yes, not much point in staying here a moment longer," said Claire.

"You have had a nice little holiday here at my expense. I hope you have enjoyed your time and have had a nice rest," said Miss Clifton, who was deeply sceptical about Claire's reason for being there.

Claire kept nibbling at her food until they all had finished eating and then she spoke. "Well we will be on our way now for we are all packed and ready to go, but before we leave I would like you all to come to the sitting room where I shall tell you all that I have found in this case."

"That won't take very long," snarled Miss Clifton, who could not wait to see Claire depart. She felt that Claire was like some kind of con man.

"If you lead the way Miss Clifton we'll follow," said Claire, in a cheerful voice. Claire was not the only one present who was enjoying the drama, for before breakfast Claire had related to Jennifer how she had rescued Percy.

When Miss Clifton came to the sitting room door she flung it open and marched right in. The room was the way it always been for many years for there was the television, the piano, the bookcase the settee all in their usual place, and of course at the window with the curtains open, was Percy standing on his perch, keeping an inquisitive eye on the group of strangers entering the room. Miss Clifton turned round and addressed Claire. "Well girl, do tell us," and then she suddenly stopped. It had at last dawned on her that there was a parrot in the room. She soon composed herself and again addressed Claire. "What is the meaning of this?"

"It's Percy," was all Claire said.

"Well I don't think so. I have known Percy for twenty eight years and I am better qualified than you to recognise Percy, and I am telling you that is not my Percy. Nevertheless, you have obviously done your best to find a replacement for my Percy which I shall accept. If you tell me how much you paid for it, I shall reimburse you. I hope you have a safe journey home. At that she went to a drawer in the room, took a key from her pocket, opened it and took out a bundle of notes.

"I didn't pay anything for it," said Claire. "It *is* Percy."

"No, it's *not.*" Miss Clifton was adamant and held out the money for Claire to take.

"I'm certainly not taking any money because I just found Percy the Parrot, and did not buy a similar one." Claire went up to the cage and started to annoy Percy, and Percy *was* annoyed. He skipped from one foot to another on his perch and then started bowing up and down, up and down with his two feet firmly gripping the perch. He was really riled. Claire waited and then Percy started up. He swore again and again, always using the same swear word mingled with Miss Clifton's name. Miss Clifton just had to pretend she was shocked and keep on lying, by saying she had never heard such swearing in all her life. "Let's return to the kitchen," suggested Claire, and this time it was she who led them.

"Well you must admit, Miss Clifton," said Claire, when they were back in the kitchen, "that the parrot looks like Percy, talks like Percy and his cage is the same one as before. We can safely say it is indeed Percy. We shall be leaving now." Claire then walked over to the backdoor, opened it and headed for Mrs Flowers' car, followed by Mrs Flowers and Jennifer.

CHAPTER 11
The Big Reward

On the journey home Mrs Flowers was completely dumbfounded by what had just occurred. Claire was the first to speak. "Do you think I was too harsh on your friend when Percy began to swear?" Claire asked.

"Not at all, Claire. I was shocked by her behaviour. She wanted her parrot back, but when she walked into the sitting room and saw Percy she was unwilling to eat humble pie, and thank you for getting him back. Then when Percy started to swear she further denied it was her parrot altogether. She will keep the parrot however, and try to pay you Claire, but she will insist that it was not her parrot for her parrot would never swear."

"I just wanted her to examine herself and see what a horrible thing pride is," explained Claire. "I really don't want her money."

When Monday morning arrived Percy the Parrot, or rather Long John Silver's parrot, was all over the local news. The story was that it had been stolen by a gang of thieves early on Sunday morning, and that after a struggle with the security guards, the gang had made their getaway on the river. The police were looking for the parrot and a substantial reward had been offered for its safe return. Pictures of Percy were all over the media and the public were urged to contact the police if they sighted the parrot.

That very morning a terrified Miss Clifton, holding the newspaper in one hand and holding Percy in his cage with her other hand, called upon her friend Mrs Flowers and begged her to look after Percy, saying that things would soon blow over, and then she would take him back home. This was great publicity for the entertainment company, but it was a nerve racking experience for Miss, who had got it into her head that the police were about to raid her home any minute and arrest her for harbouring the stolen parrot. Mrs Flowers, seeing the distress of her friend, agreed to look after Percy.

When Claire and Jennifer returned home from school that day Mrs Flowers invited them for tea in her sitting room. When they entered they could hardly believe their eyes, for there in the corner of the room was Percy in his cage, sitting on his perch giving them a wary look. "Whatever you do Jennifer and Claire, don't annoy Percy," exclaimed Mrs Flowers, when she saw the way Percy was looking at Claire. They all laughed. "I have been asked to look after Percy until things blow over," explained Mrs Flowers. The two friends understood.

"How did Percy learn to swear like that?" asked Jennifer.

"I think I know the answer to that," said Mrs Flowers. "Miss Clifton goes on holiday abroad three times a year and gets the local handyman to look after Percy."

"I understand," said Jennifer.

"She probably never knew her parrot swore until Claire upset him," said Mrs Flowers. "When was it you found it out, Claire?"

"When I was running as fast as I could with Percy in his cage getting buffeted about, with the Hound of the Baskervilles and its friends chasing me," said Claire.

Jennifer and Mrs Flowers looked across at Claire, both wondering who exactly this young girl was.

CHAPTER 12

The School Cricket Club

Jennifer used to enjoy playing cricket in the street with mainly local boys before she came to stay next to Mrs Flowers. She was good at both bowling and batting, so when she heard that the junior schools girl's cricket team were looking for new members she joined the team. During the cricket season they entered a twenty over home and away competition with other schools in the region. It was the job of the home team to supply two umpires. One to stand behind the wicket at the bowler's end, and one to stand at square leg.

Things went well with Jennifer and the team until they had a home game against a team from the local Girls' school. Jennifer's team were comprehensively beaten by them, not because they deserved to be beaten, but because of the aggressive behaviour of their opponent. When it came to bowling they now and again would aim the ball not at the wicket, but rather at the body of the girl batting.

It was Jennifer's school that was doing the umpiring that day when they were badly beaten by the Girls' school. The umpires were just senior pupils at Jennifer's school, but they did not have the courage to dismiss the bowler for her aggressive behaviour. The first time the umpire no-balled the bowler the teacher in charge of the visiting team came up to the umpires and started arguing with their decisions. She was a big woman, a sergeant major type, and that day her bullying tactics won the day. For this very match she got helped by the fact that Mr Jasper, who was the teacher in charge of Jennifer's team, had not intervened. So it ended up that Jennifer's team got well and truly thrashed.

Now, just a few days before the return match at the girls' school, Jennifer happened to mention to Claire that she did not want to go to the match, and asked if Claire could take her place. "Why don't you want to play?" asked Claire. Jennifer explained about their cheating and intimidation.

"I don't really understand why, but this I do know, Claire, that you could sort them out." Claire was humbled by Jennifer's words, and not puffed up with pride that so many others would have been.

"If you think it would help then I will join our school's cricket team on the condition that you don't give up Jennifer, but come along too. Is there anyone else in your cricket team who might give me their place in the team for just that day?"

"Oh yes, lots," answered Jennifer. "More than half the team don't want to play, but when they hear you will be in our team perhaps they will change their minds." The teacher in charge of the team, Mr Jasper from the modern languages department, had arranged a meeting, at the request of the team, that very day after lunch in his classroom. He was hoping that the team were wanting the game to be called off so he did not have to supervise them on Saturday, and he would have the whole day to himself. He did not really like taking the cricket team, but he hoped by taking the team to gain brownie points in the eyes of the headteacher. Jennifer took Claire to the meeting, where Mr Jasper had no objection to her joining the club.

Now Mr Jasper knew that the team had asked for the meeting to persuade him to call off the game, which he was only too willing to do. Imagine his disappointment when he heard they were now all keen to take part, just because Claire had joined the team. They were sure Claire could sort things out for most of them had seen Claire performing in the gym hall. The team captain, already knowing who had given up their place to Claire, picked the team and handed the list to Mr Jasper. They would all meet again on Saturday morning at nine thirty at the school, and then Mr Jasper would run them to the match in the school's minibus.

CHAPTER 13
The Cricket Match

On Saturday morning at half past ten, a coin was tossed with the result that Jennifer's team lost and were put into bat. It had been agreed that Claire and Jennifer would open the batting and Claire would take the first strike. The bowler came running up to the wicket and bowled the ball, in Claire's opinion, directly at her body. Claire waited for the right moment and gave it such a whack that it went flying over the wicket keeper's head for a six. The umpire, who had been waiting for the ball to strike Claire on her body, got such a surprise, she awarded Claire a six. The second ball was not bowled but thrown at Claire, who this time hit the ball over the head of the bowler for another six. The third ball was aimed at Claire's face and that also went for a six. The fourth ball was a bouncer aimed at hurting Claire, but Claire easily dealt with it and again it was another six.

Before bowling the fifth ball the umpire winked twice at the bowler. Claire noticed it and was sure they were up to no good at all. The bowler this time did not take a long run up but just strolled up and bowled a soft ball. Claire hit it for a six and was immediately declared to be out for striking the ball twice, once with the bat and then with her hand that was no longer on the bat, so as to change the direction of the ball. Everyone watching knew the umpire was cheating and waited to see what Claire would do. Claire did not budge causing the umpire to go berserk. She was a big girl and went marching up to Claire roaring and shouting, doing her best to intimidate her. "You're out. You struck the ball twice," she yelled, and yelled and yelled. Mr Jasper, who usually took no interest in the game had become interested when he saw Claire strike the first ball for a six. He had seen the ball being thrown at Claire and not bowled and now he had just witnessed Claire striking another six, with only one swipe at the ball. He was all riled up and he was not going to put up with this egregious behaviour any longer. He ran over to the umpire who was now in Claire's space trying to make her feel as uncomfortable as possible. The teacher in charge of the opposition team also started haranguing Claire.

"Claire, we are leaving, and you come too Jennifer," cried Mr Jasper. "I should have stopped the match the moment I saw this so- called bowler chuck the ball. We are going."

"Very well, you lose the game," called out the teacher, as she saw Mr Jasper lead the two girls back to the pavilion.

"I would rather we lose the game than one of my team lose their life. I should have ended the game sooner."

"Thank you, Mr Jasper," said Claire. "It was like a battlefield out there." When they walked into the pavilion Mr Jasper was clapped and cheered by the rest of the team.

"I hope we never have to play this team again," said the team captain.

"As long as I take the team you will never have to," said a very determined Mr Jasper.

"Three cheers for Mr Jasper," said the team captain, and the cheers made the rafters ring. They were soon back in their minibus heading for the school unaware that trouble lay ahead for Mr Jasper.

CHAPTER 14

Mr Jasper Makes a Stand

On Monday just after the morning break, Mr Jasper was summoned to the headteacher's office and another teacher was assigned to take his class. Mr Jasper went to the headteacher's office, knocked and was told to enter. There sitting behind her mahogany desk was the headteacher with her deputy, Mr Neal, by her side. Before he even had a chance to sit down the headteacher vented her anger on him. "What's this I hear of you upsetting the staff at the Girls' school? I have had the headteacher of the school on the phone telling me of your unacceptable behaviour. You ought to remember that when you take your team to another school, you are acting as a representative of this school. Your behaviour was a disgrace walking away from the cricket match just because you disagreed with the verdict of the umpire. You will immediately phone the headteacher and apologise for your outrageous behaviour." She dialled the number using the phone on her mahogany desk and held it up for Mr Jasper to take hold off.

Mr Jasper knew, along with most of the teachers in the school, that many of the local politicians sent their daughters to the Girls' school, which no one was allowed to criticise at all. "It looks like I have annoyed someone of importance," thought Mr Jasper. He just looked at the headteacher as if she were daft and turned to leave.

At this point in the proceedings, Mr Neal sprang into action and blocked Mr Jasper heading for the door. "You are not going anywhere until you get on that phone and apologise," he screamed at Mr Jasper. They both stood there trying to stare each other down. The first to blink was Mr Neal. He knew he had met his match and he let Mr Jasper leave and get back to his classroom.

Mr Jasper could hardly believe that he had stood up to these two bullies. He had seen Claire stand up to the bullies at the cricket match and that had given him the courage to do likewise. When he reached his classroom he entered with a big smile on his face, which surprised the teacher who had been looking after his class.

CHAPTER 15
The Gospel Bus

On Sunday afternoons Mrs Flowers would drive Claire and her friends to the Sunday School at their local church. Although Mrs Flowers would help the Sunday School teachers, she would often pray that she could be more of a help to the children of the district. One day she was reading the local paper when she saw an old single decker bus for sale. She prayed about it and then she bought the bus. She had the idea of driving the bus to a nearby housing scheme, where she knew that most children had never gone to a Sunday School, or knew what a Sunday School was all about. She wanted to tell them about the gospel.

The housing scheme was rather run down and so she felt the old bus was ideal as she did not want to be driving a fancy expensive looking bus into a deprived part of the town. The church members were enthusiastic about her project and gave her their blessing. The bus was adapted for the purpose and an old portable bellows harmonium , that had been in the store room of the church for over sixty years, was placed in the luggage boot at the back of the bus.

Soon the Sunday came when all were ready to set out. The driver of the bus was Mr Aldwyn, who was retired and had actually been a bus driver in his past life. Claire and her friends were among a small group of children who would be helping out, while Mrs Flowers and a group of church members were there to look after the safety of the children. Their first destination that Sunday was a patch of waste ground in the centre of the housing scheme. The portable harmonium was set up and gospel choruses were sung, attracting a small group of children who came over to see what was going on. Then it was Claire's turn. With the megaphone in one hand and the Bible on a stand she read from John's gospel.

That brought Claire to the attention of a group of youths who swaggered over to have a closer look. Their leader saw this as a good opportunity to show off, so he came right up to Claire and growled at her. "Why don't you shut up?" he yelled "You are giving us all a headache," and at the same time he tried to wrench the megaphone from Claire. He failed miserably, for Claire was ready for him. However, he did manage to knock over the stand and the Bible fell to the ground. One of his pals picked it up and handed it to him. He held it up for all to see, then ripped it in two right before Claire's eyes, hoping that it would provoke her to step down from her box and start a fight. He looked disappointed so he threw the two parts of the book to others in the gang, who ripped it up even more so pages were lying all around.

Now Claire had memorised the whole Gospel of John so she continued as if nothing had happened. That annoyed the gang greatly, so they started shouting and booing until they got fed up and slunk away, knocking over the harmonium as they departed. A young church member then gave a short sermon to the group of children who had not left. Finally a few choruses were sung with Claire playing the harmonium, which had been patched up. The children present were given the gospel of Mark as a small booklet, and a card with the invitation to attend the Gospel Bus next week at the same time.

The Gospel Bus group next started tidying up and returning the harmonium to the boot of the bus. To their surprise the group of children stayed to help gather up the pages of the Bible that were scattered around. They were being looked after by a young lady called Polly.

"Will you really be here next week, Miss?" asked one little girl, looking at Mrs Flowers who was collecting torn up parts in a plastic bag.

"Yes, we will," said Mrs Flowers, who was surprised at being asked. Mrs Flowers looked down at the little girl and smiled. "May I ask your name?"

"Yes. I'm Lyn, and this is my little brother Malcolm

and that's my big brother Cameron over there. She then named all the other children present. Claire took note.

"Well Lyn, we shall be here next week, God willing," said Mrs Flowers, with determination in her voice as if neither flood or fire would stop her. "I hope to see you and all your friends next Sunday."

"I'm so glad," said Lyn. "No one ever comes here. I think we are forgotten."

Soon the Gospel Bus group was all packed up and ready to go. The children who had stayed waved them goodbye and headed for home. "If it was not for that youth ripping up the Bible, then the children would not have stayed and helped tidy up the mess," said Mrs Flowers. "Now we know their names and we all will be back next Sunday, shan't we?"

"Yes," they all cried out, including Mr Aldwyn, the driver who had been listening. Mrs Flowers said a prayer of thanks and then they were ready to depart.

CHAPTER 16
A Near Tragedy

The Gospel Bus had only gone a short distance when, "Stop the bus," rent the air. It was Claire who had called out. Mr Aldwyn drew into the side of the road and Claire sprang out. The gang that had ripped up the Bible were standing on the other side of the road shouting with all their might in great distress. They were looking down at the railway line now screaming their heads off. Claire understood and acted.

There on the actual railway line lay their gang leader showing off just how brave he was while thinking he was quite safe. Little did he know there was a train coming in his direction and it looked to everyone in his gang that he was bound to die. If they had just kept quiet he may have heard the train approaching, but he was quite oblivious of what was about to happen.

Claire was by now halfway down the railway embankment doing her best to reach the boy before the train arrived. There was no time to run down any more so she just took one gigantic leap and landed beside the boy, picked him up and dived to the other side of the track. The train had arrived. | It only took a few seconds for the train to pass them by, but to those watching it seemed much longer. Now the onlookers from the bus and some that had been at the meeting, including Polly and the children, had to wait to see if Claire had been successful in rescuing the boy. To the gang it looked as if both were dead, for their motionless bodies lay together at the side of the track, with Claire's body sheltering the boy. Claire suddenly jumped up and then pulled the boy up on his feet. She took him by the arm and led him across the track where they started their climb up the embankment. As they climbed Claire was the first to speak. "What's your name?" she enquired.

To Claire's surprise he answered. "Brice."

"I'm Claire, by the way. It's nice to meet you." It was then Claire was moved to give him her mobile number. Now Claire had a collection of mobile phones and the number she gave him was not that of her personal phone, but rather just a phone she would use in unplanned circumstances like the one she was in now. Claire wrote the number down on the back of a card and handed it to Brice.

"Thank you, Claire, and thank you for saving my life," said Brice, who surprised Claire by his pleasant attitude. When they reached the top of the embankment Claire presented him to his friends, who were standing on the road, across from the

Gospel Bus. Claire simply crossed the road, went into the bus, collected a bundle of Mark's Gospel and invitation cards to the Gospel Bus' services, and handed out the gifts to the gang.

By now the bus had emptied for they all had come out to see what on earth was going on. What they did see was the gang members thanking Claire when she handed them the gifts. Most of the Gospel group were wondering why they did not rip them up and throw them away. When they got back into the bus and Mr Aldwyn slowly drove away, every member of the gang waved goodbye.

In the bus they all kept looking at Claire in amazement wondering what had happened. "God helped me to get that boy to safety," was all that Claire said. Mrs Flowers prayed and thanked God for the amazing time that they had. When they arrived back at the church they also all thanked Mr Aldwyn, had lunch together and then got ready for the Sunday School which was to meet at three o'clock.

CHAPTER 17
The Tip Off

On Tuesday morning of that same week, Claire received a text message from Brice, the gang leader whose life Claire had saved. The message was brief and to the point. That very night there was going to be an attempt to burn out the Gospel Bus by a gang of armed drug dealers. After school, Claire sat in her chair and made sure she was fully charged and then prepared for the night to come. She knew she would be making one phone call to the police so she got ready a phone with a new SIM card which she would probably only use once. That night she left her bedroom via the window and made her way to Mrs Flowers'. When Claire and Molly had fixed Mrs Flowers' fence, they had left a secret gap in it. Claire went through the cap and was soon to be found in Mrs Flowers' front garden. Some time later, two grown up thugs arrived and parked outside Mrs Flowers' front garden. They got into the garden by cutting away part of the front garden fence and then made their way to the Gospel Bus parked on the driveway. Both of them were carrying a large can of petrol and a bitumen type torch on a pole about a metre long. Claire would normally have come out of her hiding place and attacked them, but as they probably had guns she decided to wait to see if there would be a safer option.

"I'm going to enjoy this," said one of the men, as they laid down their bitumen torches and opened their petrol cans and started to splash the petrol all over the bus the best they could. When the petrol landed on the side of the bus some of it rebounded and landed on the thugs. They obviously had forgotten, or never heard of Newton's Third Law of Motion. The more the can emptied the easier it was to throw the petrol on the side of the bus, but the bigger was the splash back. When they had finished their work both were covered in petrol but thought nothing of it, as the whole place already stunk of petrol.

"I'm enjoying this night," said one of them.

"Better than sitting in the pub," said the other. "The old fool deserved it."

One of them picked up the two torches and started to use his cigarette lighter to set the torches burning. To begin with it started as dim light but it was soon turned into a raging, roaring flame. It was then when the arsonist with two torches was about to hand his accomplice his torch, that Claire acted.

She placed her two hands in the shape of a megaphone around her mouth and made the following announcement in a loud voice. "This is the police. Place your hands above your head." The two gangsters got such a fright on hearing the word police that they reached for their guns, so that the torches went flying. One landed at the feet of one of the arsonists, while the other torch hit the sleeve of the other one, resulting in his petrol soaked sleeve going up in flames. He had reached for his gun, but when he saw he was now on fire he lost his calm, went berserk and dropped his gun. He ran over to the front lawn and started to roll around hoping that would smother the flames, but to no avail for all his clothing was now alight.

CHAPTER 18

Claire Tries to Help

Claire ran over to a bush, ripped a leafy branch from its side and went over to the man who was screaming on the lawn. Using the branch she did her best to beat out the flames, but it made no difference. He stopped screaming for now he was dead. She turned round to find out what was happening to the other gangster and discovered he had got to his feet, but he too had now caught alight. His shoes were on fire and the bottom of his trouser legs. He was pointing his gun in the direction of Claire when he suddenly realised his plight. He dropped his gun and concentrated on getting rid of his trousers.

The flames had now leapt up as high as his waist and his belt. He tried to undo his belt, but it only resulted in his sleeves catching alight. He ran towards the porch screaming all the way. He just managed to climb the steps and press the bell before he fell back down the steps and died. Claire returned to her hiding place to phone for help, when suddenly she looked up and saw a light from an upstairs bedroom of the house, and there stood Mrs Flowers with her phone to her ear. "She must be phoning the police," said Claire, when she looked up. "I wonder how long she has been standing there? I think it's time for me to leave."

As Claire went to leave suddenly she stopped dead in her tracks, for a frightening thought had entered her mind. "When I heard one of them say, *the old fool deserved it,* I should have asked myself, *deserved* what? I thought they were talking about Mrs Flowers, but more likely they could have been talking about Mr Aldwyn, for the past tense of the word deserve had been used. If they put him out of action there will be nobody to drive the bus or any replacement. I think they must have already visited him."

She wasted no time and phoned Mrs Flowers. She got through immediately and was brief. "This is Claire Mrs Flowers. Can you hear me?" asked Claire hurriedly.

"Yes, I can."

"When the police arrive I want you to get one of them to take you immediately to Mr Aldwyn's house. I think he may be in great danger, or these thugs that tried to burn the bus have already visited him. There is no time to lose, you must go as soon as you can. You know, of course, not to mention my name," and so saying she ended the call. As Claire made her way back to her home she justified to herself the request she had just made to Mrs Flowers. "These people will probably not give up until they stop the Gospel Bus entering their territory. They see the housing estate as their dominion, where they alone rule and they certainly don't want the Gospel Bus anywhere near them. They will do *anything* to stop us," thought Claire. It was the "do anything," that frightened Claire. "They may have killed Mr Aldwyn before coming here so there would be no one to drive the bus."

Mrs Flowers, having opened the gates to her driveway, was actually by now in the front garden, awaiting the police. She had thought over what Claire had said, and she too now believed Mr Aldwyn was in great danger. When the police arrived Mrs Flowers told her fears to the sergeant. He agreed with her and sent a woman constable to Mr Aldwyn's home taking Mrs Flowers along with her. When they stopped outside Mr Aldwyn's house, Mrs Flowers jumped out of the police car and ran up the garden path. She gave out a cry of pain when she saw what she did not want to see. There lying on the doorstep with the door still open was Mr Aldwyn badly beaten up. An ambulance was called and the sergeant was informed. When he arrived a short time later to see for himself, he went over to Mrs Flowers and addressed her in a calm voice.

"Looks to me our two suspects first paid a visit to your friend Mr Aldwyn before they came calling to your house, Mrs Flowers. "Perhaps I'm not supposed to say this." He bent his head and groaned. "I'm sorry, so sorry, that these two young men have died and their families have been deprived of a son, but I am glad they cannot harm anyone ever again."

The ambulance had already arrived and was now ready to take Mr Aldwyn to hospital. Mrs Flowers went with them and on the way phoned Claire to fill her in on what had been happening. Mrs Flowers never did ask Claire what she had been up to in her front garden that night, and no one ever found out what Mrs Flowers had seen from her bedroom window that same eventful night. She told the police that she had heard the screaming, which was true, and that was all she was prepared to say.

CHAPTER 19
They Would not be Deterred

By Wednesday evening what had happened that night was the talk of the town. Round the kitchen table after their evening meal, Claire and the rest talked about the Gospel Bus. "The Gospel Bus was a great way of getting the gospel to places that had never heard the gospel," said Mrs Low. "Do you think now that the attack on Mr Aldwyn and then the attempt to destroy the bus will put an end to the visits of the Gospel Bus, Claire?" She asked Claire because she knew Claire and her friends had been on the bus when it visited the housing estate.

"If Mum permits me, I certainly will be going on the Gospel Bus and visit the same place as last week, and Mrs Flowers has told the children, that God willing, we will be back."

"I will not be stopping you, Claire," said her mother, and she meant it. "The Church cannot give into threats like those we witnessed the other night. By the way, does anyone know how Mr Aldwyn is doing?"

"He is still in intensive care," said Bella. "I think it

is going to be difficult to find a replacement driver for the bus. Let's pray for him right now. So they all bowed their heads as Bella prayed earnestly.

"There will be a meeting tomorrow evening in the church about the future of the Gospel Bus," said Claire, after the prayer had been said. "Mrs Flowers is going and she says she will take me there if you approve, Mum."

"Of course you may go, Claire."

A short time later Claire received a text from Brice saying that if the Gospel Bus was coming back on Sunday then his big brother, Boyd, was quite willing to stand in for Mr Aldwyn. Claire phoned him and accepted the offer. She also learned that Mr Aldwyn was a well known figure in the housing estate having been the school bus driver for that area. He was still much loved and the assault on his person had caused much anger among the residents. "They had picked on the wrong person this time," said Brice, at the end of the call. Claire then texted Mrs Flowers and told her the good news about the driver offer.

Mrs Flowers did run Claire to the meeting the following evening where they got an up to date information on the progress of Mr Aldwyn. He was still in intensive care and prayers were said for him. Mrs Flowers then told the meeting about what had happened in the attempt to burn the bus and how the thugs had been thwarted. Claire had not told anyone about her role in the affair, so Mrs Flowers' version was just what the police had told her, and she was not going to add anything else. She told those present that the bus had not been damaged, and now because they had found a driver they would be returning to the housing estate again on Sunday.

However, the pastor of the church was against returning and said the church would not give its backing to such an irresponsible act of stupidity. The meeting then broke up with Mrs Flowers not at all pleased with the outcome, and Claire wondering just what type of pastor the church had. "Out of the three Cs, is he a cowardly pastor, a complicit pastor or a courageous one?" she asked herself.

In the Church's car park the young man and the young women, Stuart and June who had been on the first outing in the Gospel Bus, came over to speak to Mrs Flowers and Claire. "We both are with you, Mrs Flowers. We'll be there on Sunday if you want us?" said June.

"We certainly do," said Mrs Flowers. Arrangements were made where to meet on the upcoming Sunday. They then went on their way, this little band of volunteers.

CHAPTER 20
The Gathering Storm

On Sunday after the morning church service, the Gospel Bus crew gathered at Mrs Flowers' mansion where the Gospel Bus was parked. True to his word, Brice along with his big brother Boyd, had turned up. Big usually meant elder brother but in this case it had a double meaning for Boyd was a big bear of a man, a person not to tangle with.

Now that all were present Mrs Flowers ushered them all into the dining room and they all sat down around the table and prayers were made for the success of their mission and grace was said. After they had eaten Mrs Flowers brought up the question of what name they should call their little group of volunteers. After much prayer she had come up with the suggestion of calling themselves the Gospeltears. "I have chosen the name gospel because our job is to spread the gospel, and the name tears because the Lord Jesus Christ wept when He saw Jerusalem." All present agreed it was a splendid name and would be happy to be called a gospeltear. It was now time to get on their way and set up the children's meeting. When the little band of gospeltears were all aboard the bus, Boyd climbed into the driver's seat and soon they were on their way.

When they arrived at their destination, they found Polly waiting for them with the same group of children that were present last time, who gave a big cheer when the bus arrived. It was then that the followers of Brice turned up. Brice and his gang stayed but Boyd left saying he would be close at hand if needed. The service began with a chorus sung by June and Stewart, with Claire on the harmonium and Mrs Flowers looking after the welfare of the children, like a hen looking after her chicks under her wing.

Mrs Flowers sensed danger when she saw some shifty men starting to hang around and ushered Polly and children, along with the gospeltears, into the safety of the bus. Brice and his followers were sent into the Gospel Bus to help with the children. Claire stayed outside the bus to guard it and Mrs Flowers oddly did not object. Claire agreed to keep in touch with Mrs Flowers by phone. It was not difficult for Claire to hide herself on that piece of waste land as there was plenty of rubbish lying around, like old wardrobes, fridges and cookers just to mention a few. She was to soon find out that she was not the only person hidden from view. The gospeltears soon had the children singing their hearts out inside the bus.

There was now a gang of ten thugs hanging around the bus, looking rather menacing. It was then Brice left the bus with his friends, who looked no match for the gang of ten thugs, who were all grown men. They reminded Claire of the two thugs who had tried to burn the bus and had beaten up Mr Aldwyn.

Then Boyd reappeared, but not alone. He had brought his gang along with him who looked as if they could handle themselves. They had come to sort out the group of ten drug dealers. The ten looked sly and street wise, but were not nearly as tough looking or as big as Boyd's gang.

Boyd and his gang did not want drugs and drug dealers in their patch. Their brothers and sisters went to school there, their mothers went to the local shops and their grandparents all knew one another. They had learned what had happened to Mr Aldwyn and did not like it at all. They all knew Mr Aldwyn for he was the school bus driver for the district, and when he retired he was one of the local lollipop men. Pity help anyone who would mess with Mr Aldwyn. Boyd's gang had a cause, and that cause was to avenge the life threatening attack on Mr Aldwyn. It was that which had brought the gang there that day, plus getting rid of the drug dealers once and for all.

The drug dealers too had a cause, and that was to avenge the death of their two companions who had been burnt to death in their attempt to destroy the Gospel Bus. They had never before gathered together in public, but now driven by hatred and revenge they had made the fatal blunder of assembling together. This gave their opponents the opportunity to get rid of them once and for all.

CHAPTER 21
The Gang of Ten

The group of ten drug dealers now felt in danger from Boyd's gang that seemed to surround them. Two of the drug dealers produced their guns and were about to shoot their way out of trouble. They pointed their weapons and took aim but never did manage to pull the trigger. The almost silent sound of two rifles each firing a bullet rang out and the two thugs fell down dead. It was Sunday afternoon with no police to be seen, for the pastor of the church had assured them that the gospeltears would not be returning. The remainder of the drug gang panicked, pulled out their guns and ran but did not get very far. It was a gang war that did not last very long. There on the waste ground lay the dead bodies of the ten drug dealers shot dead by the very same snipers who had just killed two of them. Beside the dead lay a couple of petrol cans and bitumen torches that they had brought along with them. The war appeared to be over for now.

In the bus the children had no idea of what had just happened, for there were blinds on the windows to prevent them from being distracted. Also there was no sound of rifle fire, for the snipers had used silencers. From her hiding place Claire saw men starting to stuff the ten bodies into a van that one of the drug dealers had arrived in. "Frank, when you are finished drive the van with the dead to the cliff," ordered Boyd. "We'll put it over the edge and then I'll drive you back in that black car beside that old fridge." The nine other cars were claimed as spoils of war and were destined to end up overseas. As the bodies were being dumped in the van, Claire crept over to Boyd's temporary black car, opened the back door and hid herself under a blanket on the back seat of the car.

"We have at last got rid of that scum who have ruined the lives of so many and have caused the deaths of so many in this district," Claire heard Boyd tell his gang just a few minutes later." Now let's leave without drawing attention to ourselves. Frank will go first and I'll follow. Don't all of you leave at once." Boyd then got into the black car. Frank drove off first, then Boyd followed, unaware that he had a passenger in the back seat.

It did not take long to get to the cliff top. Frank parked the car facing the sea on the slope down to the cliff edge. Boyd went over to help Frank push the van. Soon it was on its way down the slope gathering speed as it went. Over the edge of the cliff it went to smash on the rocks below never to be seen again. Claire, who had seen it all, hid once again under the rug in the back seat. Boyd was soon back in the black car heading for the Gospel Bus with Frank sitting next to him in the passenger seat and Claire hidden under a blanket in the back seat.

When they got back to the bus, Boyd and Frank got out of the car and went over to Frank's car. They chatted for a few minutes and then Frank joined the rest of the gang, but Boyd went over to the Gospel Bus to collect Brice. When he got there he found Claire sitting alone on the steps onto the bus.

"Hello. Boyd," said Claire. "I'm so glad you have decided to visit us." He wasn't given time to respond, for Claire had grabbed hold of his hand, dragged him up the steps and into the bus. Before Boyd knew what had happened he found himself standing next to Mrs Flowers who in no way was going to let him leave until the service had ended. Claire went back out and sat once more alone on the steps of the bus. No one really noticed Claire had not been present for the past twenty minutes, for Brice had done a good job looking after the children which Claire should have been doing.

When it was time to leave the gospeltears promised to be back next week, and Polly made sure that the children all got home safely. Boyd drove the Gospel Bus, along with Brice and the gospeltears, back to Mrs Flowers' house and parked it in the driveway next to his actual car which also happened to be black. Mrs Flowers thanked Boyd for driving the bus and taking Mr Aldwyn's place.

"Anytime you need a driver for the bus let me know, Mrs Flowers." She thanked him. "Let's go, Brice," he called out to his younger brother.

"I was thinking of helping Mrs Flowers at the Sunday School, Boyd," replied Brice.

"OK," called Boyd, as he drove off alone without saying another word, for he was so surprised at Brice's behaviour, that he was lost for words. Mrs Flowers, Brice and the gospeltears then drove to the church to get ready for the Sunday School.

The Pastor was there and he went over to see Mrs Flowers. "I'm so glad Mrs Flowers that you have given up the silly notion of taking the Gospel Bus into that lawless, drug ridden housing estate." Mrs Flowers just smiled and said not a word as she and Claire headed to the Sunday School classrooms along with Brice. The other gospeltears arrived in their cars a few minutes later and were soon ready to start another lesson. |Among the gospeltears only Claire knew what had really happened that eventful Sunday afternoon.

That night, as Claire sat charging, she thought of the families involved in the whole mess that she herself had a part in. The one thing the drug dealers did not want or needed was a group of people preaching against drugs. They had to be stopped and they were the ones to stop it, but now their families would never see them on the face of the earth again. On the other hand Boyd and his gang were defending their families from the scourge of drugs. They had seen their families, and their friends' families being deprived of their loved ones and had had enough. "Surely there could have been other ways of stopping the drug trade in that area," said Claire, with a sad heart.

CHAPTER 22
Molly's Missing Pony

A pony had been stolen from a young family who lived in a large detached house near Mrs Flowers. After asking around for advice as to what to do about the theft, the grandfather of the children whose pony was stolen, came to Mrs Flowers for help. Molly was contacted and arrived the next day at Mrs Flowers' just after ten in the morning having been driven there by Joe. Mrs Flowers had suggested that the children, Gemma and Tommy also come and her wish had been granted. The children were to play an important part in recovering the pony, unknown yet to Mrs Flowers. On Friday morning Molly paid a visit to the grandfather of the children and found out as much as she could about the pony, and how and when it had been stolen.

That very same day after school, Claire was helping in the kitchen with the rest of the staff to prepare the evening meal, when there was a knock at the back door. Claire answered it and got a big surprise, for there, standing appearing to be on their own, were Tommy and Gemma. Claire put her index finger to her lips as a signal for the children to be quiet. "Someone at the door to see you, Mrs Low," called out Claire, and then went back to her work after leaving the door ajar. Mrs Low left her cooker, went to the door and pulled it open.

"Goodness!" exclaimed Mrs Low, when she saw the two little ones standing there alone and smiling. "You better all come in and that includes you Molly." Molly emerged from round the corner with a big smile on her face.

"How did you know I was there, Mrs Low?" asked Molly.

"You are not the only detective hereabouts," said Mrs Low, with a grin.

"Here's your custard jar back, Mrs Low," said Gemma, who had been hiding it behind her back. "and thank you everyone for the custard and the pies," continued Gemma, as she handed the jar back to Mrs Low. It was only a short visit for Molly and the children had to get back to Mrs Flowers' mansion, and prepare for the evening meal and the children's bedtime. Next day was Saturday, for Molly had timed things nicely, so Claire was invited to come round and visit Molly.

Molly filled Claire and Mrs Flowers in on the details of the case. "I believe the pony is with some other stolen horses around here. I asked the grandfather where they went to get supplies for the pony, like food and straw. They ordered their supplies on the internet from the Radcliffe company who delivered it to them and carried it to the pony's stable. I did some research on the Radcliffe family and found they provide pony rides to young children, but they charge a lot of money for just five minutes. I think there is a good chance of finding the stolen pony at the Ratcliffe farm, but I need help from both of you."

"How exciting," exclaimed Mrs Flowers, who loved helping Molly.

That very morning found Claire, Molly and the children being driven by Mrs Flowers to the Radcliffe farm, not to buy anything, but to give the children a pony ride. "I've brought my microchip reader with me, the one you bought for me, Mrs Flowers," explained Molly as they travelled to the farm.

"You're not telling me that ponies have microchips in them too?" asked Mrs Flowers.

"Yes, they do have them, and I shall be able to tell if the pony I'm looking for is at this farm."

"Well, I never have!" exclaimed Mrs Flowers. "I thought it was just for dogs and cats."

"All I have to do is find this pony, for the police have told the grandfather that if the pony is found they will go and collect it for him. The police think the pony is now hundreds of miles away, but I think it's at the farm we are going to.

On arriving at the farm Mrs Flowers booked a pony ride for each of the little children. Gemma went first. She was given a safety helmet and then given a five minute ride around the paddock with a helper at her side. Photos could be taken and that is exactly what Mrs Flowers and Molly did.

At the end of the ride more photos were taken standing next to the pony and hugging and fussing over it. Mrs Flowers also took photos of Molly hugging the pony and petting it, although that was not what she was actually doing. The attendant was paying no or little attention to what was going on. What Molly was actually doing was locating the microchip and then reading its ID number using her hand-held microchip scanner. Then Tommy had his five minute turn around the paddock on the other pony. Photos again were taken and again Molly using her hand-held scanner read off the ID number. She had found the pony that she had been hired to find. It was now getting busier and other small children were arriving to see the ponies.

After paying for the children's pony ride, Mrs Flowers ushered everyone into her car and drove back to her home. There they went into the sitting room and discussed what had to be done next. "I thought we might have to steal back the pony one night, but I think it is just a job for the police," said Molly. Indeed Molly was correct. She paid a visit to the grandfather, told him she had found the pony and where it was to be found. The grandfather met up with the police, who using their own scanner identified the stolen pony and it was soon back with the grandfather and his grandchildren.

CHAPTER 23

The Invitation

One Friday afternoon after school when Claire arrived home and was helping in the kitchen her phone rang. It was from Sir Robert Buchanan. He asked Claire if she could come to his home city to play in a concerto this Saturday evening. Claire set the sound level on her phone so all in the kitchen could hear Sir Robert. He explained to Claire that the famous virtuoso they had booked had taken ill and asked if she could take his place. "If you can come right away I shall send my chauffeur along with my niece Jane, to pick you up. You can bring a friend or friends if you want for I have reserved seats for you in the front row," said Sir Robert. All in the kitchen had stopped working and were gazing at Claire. "Do you think you will be able to come?" asked Sir Robert.

"May I?" Claire asked her mum, who nodded her consent.

"Are you sure you will all manage without me if I go, for there is to be a dinner party tomorrow evening?" asked Claire.

"We'll manage all right, Claire", said Mrs Low, "but we are all going to have to work a little bit harder, and of course we shall miss you, who here wouldn't? Now you tell Sir Robert you will be coming."

"What do you want me to play, Sir Robert?" asked Claire.

"Well you choose, Claire. It's either Rachmaninov Piano Concerto No 3, or Tchaikovsky Piano Concerto No 1. We have been rehearsing both."

"Can I really choose?" asked Claire.

"Of course you can. What you choose we will play."

"Then I choose both. Why not begin with the Rachmaninov and if I get an encore we can play the Tchaikovsky. That is, of course, if I do get an encore."

"Oh I am sure you will," said an amazed Sir Robert. "Why did I not think of that?" So Sir Robert was delighted and his chauffeur was sent to pick Claire up along with Jane.

"I wish I could take you all with me," said Claire.

"Why not ask your school friends and Molly to go with you, Claire?" suggested Bella.

"There are complications," said Claire. "Molly has a Saturday job. If I ask her to be my guest at the concerto she would have to say yes, I suppose, and she would not get paid that Saturday."

"I think it's best not to ask her to come," said Mrs Low. "If you did ask her, then knowing Molly she would feel obliged to go." Claire thought it wise not to phone Molly, so she decided to phone her school friends. It turned out that Rosie and Eleanor were required to help on the farm that day and Judith's parents did not give her permission to go at all. As for Jennifer, Claire had told her that she would be coming to support her in her cricket match on Saturday afternoon, so she had to phone Jennifer and tell her that she would be not attending. Jennifer sounded very upset at the news, for she had been chosen to play in the county junior team. Claire and Mrs Flowers had been very much looking forward to seeing her play in her debut match which was indeed a great honour.

All those in the kitchen had heard Claire on the phone and were disappointed that she would have none of her friends with her. "I shall be alright alone, and besides Sir Robert's niece, who is coming with the chauffeur to collect me, will be looking after me. Nevertheless, when I walk out onto the platform I shall be thinking of you all. You will be there with me in my heart." All present in the kitchen seemed to cheer up at Claire's words and were assured all would go well for Claire.

"You run along now and get ready for the chauffeur coming to pick you up," said Claire's mum.

"I shall go and get packed now." Soon Claire was heading in Sir Robert's chauffeur driven car to the city hotel where she would spend two nights. She soon got chatting with Sir Robert's niece, Jane, who explained what was going on.

"We don't think the pianist who was meant to be playing is ill at all," explained Jane. "It is funny that he fell ill when all other well known pianists are engaged in other countries. He has probably done it as a publicity and sympathy stunt. That is what most of us think. All the ticket money has been refunded, but the hall is still booked. The orchestra has lost a lot of money on the deal, but we are going to go ahead with the concerto and try and break even. If it had not been for you Claire stepping in at the eleventh hour all would have been lost. So thank you."

"I remember that happening before," said Claire, "and that is how I first met your uncle. We know that all things work together for good to them that love God."

CHAPTER 24

Claire's Big Surprise

Saturday morning arrived to find Claire all alone in a hotel room in central London. She had breakfast alone, but later she was to be joined by Jane when it was time to go to rehearsals. At the same time Claire was having breakfast, so was Jennifer, also alone. When it was time for Jennifer to go to the county cricket ground, Mrs Flowers drove her there. It had now started to rain, and shortly after arriving at the cricket ground, to the disappointment of both of them, the match had to be called off. On the other hand rehearsals went well for Claire that morning and now all was ready for the evening concertos.

Just a few minutes before eight o'clock that evening in the concert hall, there was to be found Sir Robert Buchanan along with Claire. They were standing together at the side entrance to the stage ready to go on and join the orchestra which had just finished tuning up. At eight o'clock precisely the side door opened and in walked Claire followed by Sir Robert. There was no cheering or clapping until Sir Robert appeared and he was cheered all the way to the podium. As Claire headed to the piano she said a silent prayer asking God for His help. After shaking hands with the first violinist she sat down at the piano and got ready to start.

The hall was packed full with mostly young students from the colleges and universities in the city. The truth was they just could not turn down a bargain, the bargain being that for a modest sum of money they now could enjoy a live performance of a piano concerto conducted by the famous Sir Robert Buchanan. If it turned out to be a flop then the audience would only have lost hardly any money, but if it was a success it would be a splendid time for them all. To most of the audience it looked like it was set to be a flop and a big one at that.

As Claire sat and looked around the hall, she just for a moment thought she recognised two people sitting side by side. That caused her to look again, and there in the audience was a girl sitting beside an older lady. "It's Jennifer and Mrs Flowers!" exclaimed Claire out loud in surprise. Both waved up at Claire who waved back as a very large smile appeared on her face, just at the same time as a similar smile appeared on the faces of her friends.

The conductor, Sir Robert Buchanan, looked over at Claire to see if she was ready to start. Claire started to concentrate while not noticing three more of her friends sitting in reserved seats in the front row next to Jane, Sir Robert's niece. Claire nodded to Sir Robert to tell him she was now ready to start. The conductor raised his baton and then the orchestra started to play followed by Claire a few moments later. Her two friends had never heard her play in an orchestra and were quite amazed at her skill. Seeing Claire sitting at the grand piano right at the front of the platform, with the audience in awe of her talent, actually made them glad that the cricket match had been called off.

CHAPTER 25
Bella's Big Surprise

Meanwhile, back at Mrs Goodyard's mansion the staff were busy getting ready for the dinner party, while their guests were being welcomed by Mr and Mrs Goodyard in the large sitting room. They were mostly business men and women, but the guest list always included others from different backgrounds. This helped improve the conversations so it was not just one topic. One of them was actually a famous violinist who was looking at the large television screen on the wall. He approached Mrs Goodyard and asked if they subscribed to a certain TV service and found they did. "Do you mind if I turn on your smart television for just a moment to see if I can spot any of my friends?" he asked Mrs Goodyard. "It won't take long and I will keep the sound down."

"Of course you may," said Mrs Goodyard, and showed him where the remote was kept. In no time at all he had the orchestra he was looking for on the big screen on the wall.

"It seems they have found some amateur pianist

to take the place of the absent celebrated virtuoso pianist," said the commentator, in a rather disparaging tone of voice. "I just hope she is not going to make a fool of herself. I would have thought that an experienced conductor like Sir Robert Buchanan would have known better, but I suppose the show must go on, and making money is more important than keeping up standards." He kept on moaning and groaning as the camera kept focusing on Claire. If he had just listened to the music and Claire's contribution to it, he would not have made such a fool of himself. He had spoken before thinking.

The television was just about to be switched off when the cry of "Stop," was heard throughout the room. Everyone turned and looked at Bella, who had been serving light non alcoholic refreshments, from behind a trolley. "I'm sorry Mrs Goodyard," said Bella, "I got carried away," and then she turned and looked at the television screen. Mrs Goodyard followed Bella's eyes and to her surprise there was Claire on the screen sitting playing the piano. Claire had changed her hairstyle hoping not to be recognised just in case anyone from her school was watching, but she could not fool Mrs Goodyard or Bella. "Just take your drinks with you and Bella will show you to the dining room. The guests followed Bella into the dining room leaving Mrs Goodyard alone in the sitting room, but not for long, as Bella soon was back leaving the guests in the capable hands of Mr Goodyard.

"I'm sorry I called out," said Bella, looking rather shamefaced.

"It's quite alright. I would have done the same thing and nearly did," said Mrs Goodyard. "Press the record button then let's go to the kitchen, but don't mention Claire's name." When they arrived at the kitchen door, Mrs Goodyard knocked and entered. She did not usually enter the kitchen before a dinner party and the staff were quite surprised at her appearance. "Are you ready to serve dinner now?" asked Mrs Goodyard.

"Yes we are," answered Claire's mum, who was in overall charge. "Mrs Low has things being kept warm in the oven to be served anytime you like."

"Bella just wants to show you something in the sitting room that you all may be interested in. It was Bella who was the first to discover it, so I'm letting Bella show you what she has found. It will only take a minute of your time, and now I must leave to see to the needs of our guests in the dining room." Bella led the way followed by Mrs Low and Claire's mum.

When they came to the closed sitting room door Bella opened it and beckoned the others to enter. They looked around the room and immediately spotted the television. There on the big screen was Claire playing the piano and close by on his podium was Sir Robert Buchanan, with baton in hand, conducting the orchestra.

"Well I never did!" exclaimed Mrs Low.

"Thank you God," said Claire's mum out loud, for she knew that it was God who had brought success to Claire. Some would say that Claire's mum should be full of pride, but she preferred to be humble. She knew *pride cometh before a fall*," and she had always avoided pride and its sister self-esteem.

She glanced over at Bella who got the message. "Time to get back to work now," said Bella, and she led the way back to the kitchen.

Meanwhile back in the concert hall, it seemed to Claire's two friends, Mrs Flowers and Jennifer, that time went too quickly for they could sense the music was coming to an end. When the orchestra and Claire ended together with a flourish, Claire sprang from her seat and shook hands with Sir Robert and then the first violinist. As the audience were clapping and cheering, Sir Robert motioned for the orchestra to stand and take a bow. Claire then bowed and left the stage followed by Sir Robert. The audience kept on clapping and cheering for they seemed to want Claire back to perform an encore and many were actually calling for one.

"I knew you were going to get an encore, Claire," said Sir Robert, as they stood in the wings listening to the cheering. "You walk on now, Claire. I shall follow once you are seated at the piano." Claire walked on to the cheers and clapping and then to an even bigger cheer when she sat down again at the piano. Then Sir Robert came back on stage and stepped up onto the podium, causing the audience to wonder what he was going to do now. For the second time in the evening he raised his baton to start a great concerto. The orchestra started to play followed by Claire on the piano, so that when the audience realised what was happening the hall rang out with the biggest cheer of the evening.

CHAPTER 26

Praise for Mrs Low

When the Tchaikovsky ended there were several cries of bravo. The audience cheered and cheered, but this time there were no cries of encore for they felt it would be unfair to ask Claire for another encore, and besides they felt emotionally exhausted after experiencing such an event. When the hall began to empty, Claire went down to the auditorium to meet her friends. She did not find her three friends who had been sitting in the front, but she knew that they soon would be found. She did find Mrs Flowers and Jennifer, who told Claire about the cricket match being called off. Claire thanked them for travelling all that distance just to come and see her. She was deeply moved by their actions.

They then went backstage where Claire introduced them to Sir Robert. "Oh, I have already met Mrs Flowers and Jennifer. I told the stewards at the entrance door that Claire's friends were to be welcomed by me before the concerto began."

"Why were they not sitting in the front row then?"

asked Claire, looking slightly puzzled.

"It was full up," answered Mrs Flowers, "so we had to sit somewhere else, somewhere you might just spot us, and you did."

"I'm glad I did spot you. It cheered me up no end just to see you." It was then Jane approached Claire telling her that some of her fans would like to meet her.

"I would love to meet them," said Claire. "Now I *wonder* who they can be?" Claire could not help but smile.

"If you would like to meet them, they are just round the bend at the foot of the corridor hoping to see you." So off went Claire and Jane and no sooner had Claire appeared round the corridor than her name filled the air and the sound of two little running feet.

Claire bent down and wrapped Gemma in one arm and Tommy in the other, and held on to them tightly. Then she lifted both up from the floor and walked down the corridor to meet Molly, who had a big smile on her face as the two friends approached each other. Claire then lowered the children and gave Molly her super hug. "I'm so glad to meet you all, but how did you get here? Don't tell me. It was Mrs Flowers and Jennifer that brought you here after you had finished work, Molly?"

Jane, who had followed Claire into the corridor, approached them with a smile on her face. "We have booked rooms for you all at a nearby hotel, as the guests of Sir Robert," said Jane. "Do you like ice cream and hot apple tart?" Jane asked the children.

"Oh, yes," both cried out, as they started to jump up and down.

"Well you can have that for pudding tonight, as long as you eat up all your carrots and greens. Now let's go and collect the rest of the gang and then head for the hotel."

"Will Sir Robert be attending?" asked Claire.

"You will just have to wait and see like the rest of us," answered Jane, with a twinkle in her eye.

Sir Robert did attend the dinner. He had booked one table in a quiet corner of the restaurant. When all had arrived and were seated, Sir Robert rose to his feet and thanked Claire for her help. He told Claire that they had broken even and had made a small profit. He added he would be sending a cheque to her, but Claire declined it. "Your hospitality to me and my friends is reward enough. I came to help out and not to make money. If I were to receive as much as one penny then that would spoil it all."

Mrs Flowers then said grace and thanked God for the food they were about to eat and for the success of the concertos. She closed the prayer by asking for a safe journey home tomorrow morning. When dinner was over Jennifer asked the little children what they thought of the apple tart. "It was very nice," said Gemma, "but Mrs Low's is just slightly better." Tommy said nothing, but nodded his approval

"Who is Mrs Low?" asked Sir Robert's niece, Jane.

"Our friend," answered Tommy. "She is very nice, just like you."

CHAPTER 27
Nancy Seeks Revenge

Now Nancy hated Claire, the reason being Claire had stopped Nancy's nasty habit of bullying children. Nancy was from a very wealthy, influential family and many at Claire's school wondered why she was not attending one of the prestigious private schools in the district. The answer was simple. Nancy was a bully and her behaviour would not have been tolerated at these schools. Here at the school where Claire attended Nancy was the Queen Bee of her year group, or at least she thought she was, until the appearance of Claire.

In the past Nancy had set her dog on Claire hoping that it would teach Claire a very fitting lesson, namely that no one messed with Nancy, but it failed badly. Claire therefore was surprised, just for a moment, when Nancy approached Claire in the playground one day, and invited Claire to have Sunday lunch with herself and her family. "Mother and father are dying to meet you, Claire," said Nancy. "Do come and join us for lunch and let bygones be bygones. Let's be friends. Do say you will come."

Claire and Nancy were in the same class for certain subjects, and recently Claire had noticed Nancy cast glances of hate towards her. Claire was therefore suspicious about the invitation. She immediately recalled the old adage *beware of Greeks bearing gifts.* "Why thank you Nancy, but surely it's my fault that we have not made up and become friends. No, you must come to my house and have lunch with us." Nancy looked angry and annoyed, but did her best to hide her feelings.

"I insist you come to *us* for lunch," said Nancy, rather abruptly unable to hide her anger at Claire's suggestion.

"I know what we can do. Let's have lunch at the local restaurant and both families can come together. What do you think of that, Nancy?" asked Claire in her small, gentle, ever so nice voice that she was so good at portraying. This further annoyed Nancy.

"See you Claire, you're just impossible. I try to make friends with you and you turn me down," said Nancy, trying her best to look reasonable, while at the same time casting Claire as some kind of trouble maker. "I am just going to ask you one more time. Will you come on Sunday to our house for lunch and meet my family or not?" Claire could see the hatred in Nancy's eyes as she asked the question.

"No, let's go to the restaurant," said Claire politely.

"Very well," growled Nancy, as she turned on her heels and left.

Claire knew that when Nancy first spoke, that Nancy was up to no good. She knew Nancy had not a charitable bone in her body and she was hiding the real reason why she wanted Claire to come to her house, a reason that would be harmful to Claire. Claire smiled because she felt that she now knew the reason. "If I go to her house, then something will be stolen, probably jewellery and I will be the number one suspect. Then she will get her friends to say she saw me burying something in the woods when I took my dogs for a walk. The police will be called and they will dig up the jewels. "Well it's not going to happen, Nancy," said Claire to herself, as she headed to her next class. "You will just have to think of something new, or go on to your plan B, but whatever you do I'll be watching and waiting." Claire there and then said an emergency prayer, asking God to keep her alert at all times, as He had just done a few minutes ago.

Claire guessed that Nancy was the type of person who looked for instant gratification and so she was expecting her to act soon. Claire was right. Just two days after their meeting in the playground, Nancy carried out her plan B.

CHAPTER 28
Plan B

It was during a gym class that Nancy swung into action. Just as they were leaving the dressing room and were heading for the large gymnasium, Nancy lingered just a moment behind the rest and slipped something into the breast pocket of Claire's jacket. When the lesson was finished, they returned to the changing room, changed and moved out to their next class when the bell sounded. This time it was Claire who lingered behind, not to do any mischief, but to speak on her own to the teacher, Miss Dexter. "Please Miss, someone has put this into the breast pocket of my jacket" said Claire, as she removed three bank notes from her breast pocket, a five, ten and twenty pound note. Claire had placed herself on red alert from Nancy and her vigilance had paid off.

"I shall just hold on to this thirty five pounds and take a note of it in the teacher's log," said Miss Dexter. "I don't think we have heard the last of this. If you need help this afternoon then send for me and I shall get another teacher to look after my class. Claire thanked her, for she was sure that someone before the end of the school day was going to accuse her of stealing their money. This someone would most likely be Nancy.

"I wonder why Nancy did not declare there and then when she was in the changing room, that she had been robbed and insist that everyone be searched?" Claire asked herself. "I suppose no one likes to be searched, and that would have made Nancy unpopular. Also it could have looked like someone who did not like me, could have taken the money and put it in my pocket so I would get the blame. No, Nancy is going to do better than that. She will try to show before a teacher that I, and I alone, was the person who took her money. I'm pretty sure Nancy thinks I have not found the money and it is yet to be stolen."

The only class that afternoon, in which both Claire and Nancy were together was the art class, and that is where Nancy carried out the next part of her plan B. Claire had just washed one of her brushes at the sink and was returning to her seat when Nancy left her seat and went towards the sink. As she passed Claire she deliberately bumped into her. "Watch where you're going you stupid idiot," yelled Nancy, and went on to call her all types of names. It took Mr Forbes, the art teacher, over two minutes to calm the situation down and get Nancy back to her seat, but the peace did not last long. "Nancy suddenly jumped up from her seat and started yelling again. This time it was more serious. "She has stolen my money. Thirty five pounds. A twenty, a ten and a five pound note," yelled Nancy, pointing her finger at Claire. "She bumped into me and picked my pocket," she screamed as she made her way towards Claire, but Mr Forbes blocked her going further. Nancy glowered at him and just stood there. "Make her empty her pockets." Mr Forbes glanced at Claire.

"I don't mind," said Claire. Nancy licked her lips in anticipation. Claire emptied all her pockets, except one. She was not going to draw attention to the breast pocket of her jacket, she was leaving that to her adversaries.

"She put something in the breast pocket of her jacket," screamed Amy, one of Nancy's friends. "I saw her doing it."

Claire removed her jacket and handed it to Mr Forbes. "Could you please search the pockets of my jacket, Mr Forbes. If I did it and found nothing, they just won't believe it," said Claire.

Mr Forbes did as requested while Nancy and her friend looked on. They were smiling at each other in expectation of what they thought was about to happen, so when Mr Forbes announced he had found nothing, Nancy and Amy went berserk.

"There must be," yelled Nancy, and grabbed the jacket from Mr Forbes and almost ripped off the breast pocket. Then she went through the other pockets and still found nothing.

"What exactly is it you are looking for?" asked Mr Forbes.

"A twenty, a ten and a five pound note. I know she took them," moaned Nancy through gritted teeth, determined to prove she was right. Claire noticed how Nancy went on about how much money it was and what it consisted of.

"It's in her bag," yelled Amy, while thinking Claire must have found the money and placed it in her own bag. Amy dashed over to the bag, grabbed it and threw it to Nancy, who emptied the contents on the nearest bench. She racked through the contents and on finding nothing she sank down on a stool exhausted.

"I think Miss Dexter, the gym teacher, will be able to help you Mr Forbes," said Claire, now that the shouting and screaming had stopped. "May I suggest you send for her immediately?" He used his smart phone and soon Miss Dexter was knocking at the classroom door. She was invited in and Mr Forbes explained the situation to her.

"Is this your money?" she asked Nancy, as she held it in front of her face. Nancy said not a word, but just scowled. "It was found by Claire in her jacket's breast pocket. I logged it in the class record book and showed it to the rest of the gym staff. Now I would like you to explain this to me Nancy, how did Claire manage to steal it from you just ten minutes ago in this very room?"

"Yes, explain also to me and the class," said

Mr Forbes, "how that can be the case. How can Claire steal money from you that Miss Dexter was holding?"

"Explain yourself," said Miss Dexter. Nancy said not a word.

"Do you want to ask anything, Claire?" asked Mr Forbes.

"I just want to ask Nancy one thing," said Claire. "Just tell me Nancy, what have I done to annoy you so that you set out to make me look like a thief?" Claire gave Nancy a searching look hoping Nancy would answer the question truthfully, but instead she lost it completely and struck out at Claire. Claire had seen the blow coming and easily dodged it. Both teachers were shocked at Nancy's behaviour causing Miss Dexter to step in and constrain her. The whole affair was reported to the school's hierarchy and it ended up in Nancy being given the standard type punishment exercise, much like the one a pupil may receive for not doing their homework or coming in late to class. On the other hand, if Nancy's plan B had come to fruition, then the police would have been involved and Claire expelled from school. After all Claire's mother was just a domestic servant, whereas Nancy's family was one of the wealthiest in the town and that justified the school's two tier punishment system.

CHAPTER 29
The Bank Holiday

A Monday bank holiday was approaching and Mrs Flowers, after praying about it with other gospeltears, decided to take the Gospel Bus to another part of town. Every Sunday they went in the Gospel Bus to the run down housing estate where they had been successful in getting local children to attend their meetings. This Monday they had agreed to take the bus to a wealthy part of the town which was in fact the very area where Mrs Flowers and Claire stayed.

On Monday morning Boyd drove the bus to the public car park of their new destination, which was next to the local playing fields. The car park was practically empty as it was mainly just used on Saturdays when the playing fields were in use. The gospeltears set up the old portable harmonium and Claire sat down to play, while a small boy operated the bellows. June and Stewart sang a selection of hymns and choruses accompanied by the Gospel Bus members.

It attracted little attention until a group of youths

from the local football club appeared who were taking the advantage of the Bank Holiday to spend some of their time training. They had already changed into their gear in a friend's garage who lived close by. To get to the playing fields they had to pass by the Gospel Bus and the singers. Now Jennifer, who was singing along with the others, had brought her Bible with her, for she was to do the first Bible reading. It was in a Bible case holder, which Mrs Flowers had bought for her and others. It was too big a temptation for one of the football team so he grabbed hold of it and threw it up into the air heading for a teammate dressed as a goalie, who was lagging behind the others. He caught it and the rest of the team cheered. "What do you think of our goalkeeper then?" asked the Bible snatcher, to the gospeltears. No one knew what to say except Claire.

"Not bad, almost as good as I am," Claire answered, as she rose from her seat at the harmonium. The whole team stopped, turned and looked at her. This dumbfounded them just for a few seconds, giving time for the snatcher to think of some kind of reply.

"OK," he shouted at Claire, "if you are that good see if you can catch it," and upon saying this he signalled to the goalkeeper to throw the bible case back to him. He immediately returned it back to the goalie and so it went to and fro between the two boys. "Come on," shouted the snatcher again. "Let's see wonder girl catch it." Claire approached them and stood in the middle of the two youths who were still throwing the case back and forth to each other.

Once again it was the snatcher's turn to throw the case to the goalie. To make sure that there was no way Claire could catch it, which would be extremely humiliating for him, he threw the case well above her head thinking he had outsmarted her. Up in the air the case went, but not high enough to be out of Claire's reach. She had anticipated what was going to happen, for she had bent down ready to use the power in her legs so as to spring up and catch the case. With one giant leap Claire caught the case and safely landed back to the ground. There was a gasp from those watching, the biggest gasp being from the snatcher. Claire drew herself up to her maximum height and marched over to Jennifer and handed her the case. Jennifer unzipped the case and took out the Bible and held it up for all to see.

Claire then turned round and found that all eyes were now on her, for they were all wondering who exactly was this young girl. Claire went right up to the snatcher and confronted him. "What's your name, please?" she asked. Without thinking he told her that his name was Rees and he was the team captain. He immediately regretted giving her the information, for after all he knew nothing about this girl. "Well Rees, I have a challenge for you and the rest of the team," said Claire.

CHAPTER 30
Claire's Challenge

Rees and his team seemed to be fixed to the spot as they waited to hear what ridiculous suggestion this girl was going to make to them. "Let's all go to the football pitch and see what you really think of my goalkeeping," said Claire. "Each of your team can take a penalty kick with me in goal, and if I save everyone of them then you have to return immediately and listen to our group for just five minutes. As a favour I shall give you *two* penalties kicks Rees, so there is no way that you could lose, or is there?"

"And what do we get if you lose?" asked Rees.

"If I lose, then if one day you cannot play Rees, for some reason or other, then I will be your substitute." They all burst out laughing.

Rees looked at his team, glanced at Claire as much as to say she must be a halfwit. "Well, what do you say to her proposal?" asked Rees, with a big grin on his face.

"Bring it on," called out one of the team, and the rest cheered to show their approval. Mrs Flowers approached Claire and gave her the same kind of look that Rees had given her just a moment ago.

"Do you know what you are doing, Claire?" asked Mrs Flowers. "We need you here to play the harmonium."

"I shan't be very long," said Claire, and so saying she went off with the football team and into the playing fields. There was a football pitch close at hand and they all went over to the nearest goal. Claire took up her position on the goal line halfway between the two posts and Rees placed the ball on the penalty spot. The team gathered round to see the young girl being humiliated, while wishing they had brought their phones with them.

Rees took a few steps back from the ball then ran up and whacked the ball sending it on its way, so he thought, into the top right-hand-side of the net, if indeed there had been a net there. The ball never reached its destination, for Claire leapt up and punched it over the bar. There was utter silence from those watching. "Do you want your second go now, Rees, or do you want to wait until later?" asked Claire, in a serious tone of voice. There was no answer. "You better send someone to collect the ball, and stay there," said Claire, as she waited for the next penalty to be taken.

The ball was collected and thrown to the next penalty taker. This time Claire saved it with both of her hands and threw it back to the penalty spot. Well this went on until everyone in the team got their chance to score, but unfortunately for them they all failed. "Do you want to take your second shot now, Rees, or do you want to stop and call it a day?" asked Claire. Rees said nothing but simply collected the ball and placed it on the penalty spot, took his run up and kicked the ball over the bar. He had planned to do that, for he did not want to be humiliated by Claire once more, saving his shot.

"Missed!" exclaimed Rees, and looked Claire straight in the eye to see if she had twigged to his deliberate miss. He groaned, for he could see he had not fooled Claire, no not for a minute. "Well a bargain is a bargain," he told his football team. "Let's go just for the five minutes that was agreed to see what this girl is all about." So they headed back to the bus with not one of them doing it reluctantly, for they all wanted to find out who this amazing goalkeeper was exactly.

You can imagine the surprise when Mrs Flowers and her crew looked round and saw Claire at the front of a group of football players leading them to the bus where they were to hear the gospel message. Mrs Flowers stood on the soap box and told those present how the Lord Jesus Christ had died on the cross to take the punishment for the sins of those that had faith in Him. Claire then mounted the soap box and told them how the Lord's righteousness was credited to all believers so they could enter heaven. Jennifer read a few Bible verses, then Claire, once more back in her seat, played the harmonium as they sang a couple of choruses. It had lasted for at least fifteen minutes and not the five minutes that had been agreed, but still no one left.

The gospel crew had planned to stay there for just about an hour, but they had actually been there for well over an hour when it was time to go. All that had attended the meeting were handed a copy of Mark's gospel with an invitation card to visit the church where they would be made most welcome.

CHAPTER 31
Molly's Case

One day, a certain Mrs Curtis visited Mrs Flowers asking for her help, because her son was being black mailed. Mrs Flowers was fast becoming the go to person if any of her friends, or friends of her friends were in trouble. Mrs Flowers immediately contacted Molly, who said she hoped to be there tomorrow morning, but added that Gemma and Tommy were being looked after by her and she would have to bring them along too.

The next morning Molly's brother Joe drove Molly and the children to see Mrs Flowers. After having been fed, Molly set off on her own to interview Mrs Curtis who lived a short distance away. Joe stayed just in case Molly was not hired by Mrs Curtis, and would have to be taken back home along with the children.

Molly soon reached Mrs Curtis' house and rang the doorbell. Mrs Curtis answered the door. "What do you want?" she snapped at Molly, when she clapped eyes on a young girl standing there all alone. "Whatever you are selling, I don't want, so you just hurry along and get out of here." Molly did not budge, even while the formidable Mrs Curtis kept on glaring at her. "Who exactly are you and what do you want?" suddenly screeched Mrs Curtis.

"I am Molly and I have been sent by Mrs Flowers to help you," answered Molly politely.

"*You!*" exclaimed Mrs Curtis. "You are Molly? You just wait there while I have a word with that Mrs Flowers." Mrs Curtis slammed the door and withdrew a short distance into the hall and phoned Mrs Flowers. From what she had just said Molly surmised that Mrs Curtis was not a personal friend of Mrs Flowers, but that someone had recommended Molly to her and to contact Mrs Flowers. Out of courtesy to Mrs Flowers, Molly just stood on the doorstep and waited, but in any other circumstance Molly would just have turned on her heels and left.

While Molly waited, Mrs Curtis was on the phone haranguing Mrs Flowers. "What do you mean sending this slip of a girl to solve a very serious blackmail case?"

"I did not recommend her, it was your friend who did. I suggest you phone her for an explanation, and at the same time ask her why she did not tell you that Molly was a young girl," said Mrs Flowers, as she ended the call.

Mrs Curtis did not like that at all for she wanted the last word, so she decided to vent her anger on Molly who was still at the doorstep. Molly gazed up at her inquiringly. "Just leave," she barked at Molly, "and tell that woman not to send you here again. A woman her age should have surely known better than to send you."

"If for the sake of your son you change your mind let me know," said Molly and left.

Molly was soon back with Mrs Flowers and Joe in the sitting room where Molly told them all that happened. The children meanwhile were being looked after by Mrs Hudson the part-time housekeeper. Joe had not yet left as he was waiting to see if Molly would take the case. "Shall we just return home, Mrs Flowers?" asked Molly. Mrs Flowers needed time to think and did not answer. "Joe can have us back home for lunch if we leave now," added Molly. Mrs Flowers was slightly disturbed by the suggestion for she had been looking forward to Molly and the children staying for a few days. They always seemed to brighten up the place.

"Oh no, don't go yet. Mrs Curtis may change her mind. I told her to phone her friend who recommended me. I shall just pay Joe now and I shall pay you for each day you stay, Molly," said Mrs Flowers rather hurriedly.

"Joe needs the money to keep his taxi business going , but I don't want any money. I shall stay here for a few days, but honestly I don't want a penny. The children love it here and to tell the truth I enjoy seeing them enjoying themselves. I'll stay with the children, that is, if you really don't mind us being here."

"Good," said Mrs Flowers. She paid Joe and he left and then she showed Molly and the children to their room.

CHAPTER 32
The Children's Holiday

When Claire came home from school that day, she got a call from Mrs Flowers inviting her round for tea in the sitting room. Such an invitation usually meant more than a cup of tea and a scone so Claire was left wondering what was behind the invitation. She went round and was shown to the sitting room by Mrs Hudson, the part-time housekeeper. Claire knocked at the door and entered. It would be hard to imagine Claire's surprise when she saw Molly and the children gazing up at her wondering who had knocked. The children jumped to their feet and ran to Claire and hugged her the best they could, before Claire bent down and picked them up, one in each arm, and took them back to their seats. Molly told Claire about her confrontation with Mrs Curtis and how they were having a short break due to Mrs Flowers' generosity.

"I think she will call and apologise, then ask you to take the case, for where else can she go for help?" said Mrs Flowers

"I think you may be right," said Molly, "but as far as apologising I have my doubts. If she does hire me I may need your help, Claire"

"Say no more Molly, I shall always be there to help you if I can. Now let's forget about the case. May I borrow your guests, Mrs Flowers and the children, and go and visit my mum and friends in the kitchen?" Mrs Flowers nodded her approval. "Mrs Low will not be talking to me any more if I don't take the children round to see her. She has been wondering when you two children will be returning her custard jar."

So Claire took them round to the backdoor of Mrs Low's kitchen. The staff in the kitchen were busy preparing the evening meal when there was a knock, knock on the outside door. "I think I know that knock," said Mrs Low, and stopped working. "Who is tapping at the door? Is that Wee Willy Winky?"

"Oh, no," came the reply.

"Well you better be in bed by eight o'clock when he comes."

"It's us. Gemma and Tommy, Mrs Low," said Gemma, who had recognised Mrs Low's voice.

"Well you better come in Gemma and Tommy," said Mrs Low, as she flung open the door. She bent down and gave both children a welcome hug. Claire and Molly then appeared.

"Tommy has brought your custard jug back, Mrs Low," said Molly. Tommy produced the jug from behind his back and handed it to Mrs Low then thanked the elderly cook.

"You really don't need to give us custard and tarts every time we leave, Mrs Low," said Molly, who did not want to take advantage of an elderly lady's generosity. The moment she said it she had wished she had not uttered a single word for the sparkle in Mrs Low's eyes seemed to vanish in an instant. "Although I have to admit the custard and tarts are the best we all have ever tasted, and we so love them and would miss not having any to take home with us," added Molly. The twinkle returned to Mrs Low's eyes, and Claire looked over at Molly and winked.

Next day was just like a holiday for Molly and the children. There had been no call from Mrs Curtis and it began to look like there would never be one. The following day was the same so Molly went to see Mrs Flowers that evening. "I think it's time to head for home tomorrow," Molly told her "We can't keep partaking of your hospitality. We had a great time, but you must admit we must be heading for home tomorrow morning."

"I understand," said Mrs Flowers, "but at least stay for lunch, and perhaps Joe will be able to join us." The next day Joe arrived just at the right time to join them all for lunch. It was while they were eating Mrs Flowers received a call from Mrs Curtis. She wanted to speak to Molly, so Mrs Flowers handed the phone to her.

"We are just about to leave, Mrs Curtis. My brother Joe is here with his taxi," said Molly.

"Put him on." Molly handed the phone over to Joe. Mrs Curtis was surprised when he answered, for she had thought Molly had lied "I'll pay the double rate for your journey here and back if you leave on your own. I shall come round right now and make sure no one will be out of pocket," and so saying she ended the call. She actually did arrive at the door five minutes later and was invited to join them. The result of the visit was Molly decided to stay and help Mrs Curtis, while Mrs Flowers along with Mrs Hudson would help look after the children.

"Are we not going home today?" asked Gemma, when Mrs Curtis had left and Joe was getting ready to leave.

"Not today," replied Joe.

"I want to go home to see my mum," said Tommy.

"I want to see Mum too, Tommy," said Gemma.

"I'll look after you," said Molly, "and Mrs Flowers and Mrs Hudson will help too."

"If Mrs Low has made us custard and tarts, then I think Mrs Low will say Joe could take it to my big brothers and sisters," said Gemma.

"I think so too," said Molly.

Molly and the children went round to see Mrs Low and the staff to tell them they were not leaving. They were disappointed that Claire was not present as she was at school. "Oh dear, we have made all this custard and tarts, but it shan't go to waste," said

Mrs Low. "I wonder if Joe could take it home and give it to your mum. Do you think Joe could do that as a big favour?"

"Oh yes, Mrs Low," came the answer from both of the children. It was then the children started to cry, for they really wanted to be home with their mother, having custard and apple tart with all the family.

"I want my mum," said Tommy.

"I want to go home too. I miss my mum," said Gemma.

Molly knew how hard her mother worked bringing up the children on her own and that is why Molly helped her mother the best she could by looking after Gemma and Tommy. It broke her heart to see them crying and she felt she was the cause of their tears. Molly looked helplessly around the kitchen wondering what she should do. It was when her eyes met the accusing eyes of Mrs Low, and the others in the kitchen that Molly realised she had made a big mistake. "Joe," said Molly, and hesitated for a few seconds, "can you take the children home to Mum, while I stay and look into the case?" Joe nodded and led the children, with one in each hand to the kitchen door. There was a smile on the face of all those in the kitchen, and also the children had stopped crying. When they reached the backdoor they said goodbye as they stepped outside. The children had indeed stopped crying but Molly did notice that Mrs Low also had shed a few tears.

All those in the kitchen took out the custard and tarts, and put them into the back of the car, which then drove off. As they headed back into the kitchen Claire's mum put an arm round Molly and gave her a hug. Molly felt much better now.

CHAPTER 33
Molly Starts Investigating

That very afternoon Molly started the investigation by interviewing Mrs Curtis at her home. Her attitude to Molly had entirely changed. She had asked around her friends who assured her that Molly was truly the best detective in the area. Now it turned out that Mrs Curtis knew who the blackmailer was, namely a young lady called Juliet. This young lady had been friendly with Mrs Curtis' son, but now she was claiming he had promised to marry her. However, about a year ago she left him for an older, much wealthier man, but they split up about a month ago. "Now she is trying to blackmail my son with these letters. My son is hoping to marry a very nice girl from an affluent family, and if these letters get into their hands then the wedding is off," said a very frustrated Mrs Curtis. It reminded Molly of the advice of a wise man. "Do right and fear no man, don't write and fear no woman." Molly kept the wise man's advice to herself, for the harm had already been done.

"Please tell me, Mrs Curtis, all you know about this

woman, where she lives, works and anything else relevant," said Molly.

"I'll do much better than that," said Mrs Curtis. "I'll take you to her house in my car at six o'clock, for then you will see her and the house. Her parents have a house in London and Juliet stays alone in the family house, which is just a few miles from here."

Soon they were in Mrs Curtis' car driving to the house. They parked on the opposite side of the road to the house, so they could get a good view of the house and garden. It was an old detached house with a stable at the back that had been used to house a horse and carriage, before motorcars were ever heard off. The whole place looked dilapidated and in need of lots of work to be done on it. "I can see why she is asking for such a large sum of money," said Claire to herself, as she eyed up the house and garden.

There was a wire mesh fence at the front of the house, cutting off access to the back garden. On both sides of the street most of the houses had walls or hedges around them. Behind the older houses on Juliet's side of the street were the local playing fields. Claire and Mrs Curtis sat in the car and waited for the appearance of Juliet. They did not have long to wait for as Mrs Curtis had predicted, just after six o'clock Juliet drove home from work, parked her car at the front of her porch, got out, opened the porch door and entered the house. "Well what do you think of her?" asked Mrs

Curtis.

"She looks very presentable indeed. I can see why your son was attracted to her."

"I'm so glad she ditched him, and went off with that wealthy old man," said Mrs Curtis. "Shall we go now, Molly?

"Not right now. It may look suspicious if we are spotted driving off, just after she arrived. Give it ten minutes and then we can leave. You can tell me more about her as we wait."

At the same time Molly kept an eye on the house and her surveillance was rewarded. Molly had spotted movement in the back garden by looking through the fence. It was Juliet and she was heading for the old stable. It was padlocked and she opened the door and entered. Two minutes later she came out and closed the padlock and disappeared back into the house. "Now that is interesting," said Molly to herself. Juliet did not appear again and so after ten minutes of waiting they drove off.

On their journey back Molly asked Mrs Curtis what type of note paper her son had used to write the letters on. "Oh", said Mrs Curtis, "he would of course have used our family stationery using a blue pen to match the logo on our note paper."

"How many letters from your son has she got hold off?"asked Molly.

"Juliet claims she has eleven letters."

"And how many letters did your son write to her?"

"He can't remember," answered Mrs Curtis.

"Could you give me a dozen blank sheets of your headed note paper, please?" asked Molly. "It's so that when I find the letters, I want to leave these sheets of blank letters in their place."

"Certainly," said Mrs Curtis, and when they arrived back at her house she collected the note paper and gave the bundle of unused sheets to Molly. Molly tore the sheets of note paper in two to show Mrs Curtis that they would not be used for writing letters.

Mrs Curtis wondered what on earth Molly was up to with this strange behaviour. She refrained from asking her in case Molly would think she was criticising her. So far she was very impressed by Molly's actions and she decided not to interfere. Mrs Curtis then delivered Molly with her sheets of note paper to Mrs Flowers' mansion, and then drove home. That evening, Molly with the help of Mrs Flowers, wrote all over the sheets of blank letters with blue pens and then tore them up into small pieces.

CHAPTER 34
Molly gets Help

Molly had arranged a meeting with Claire and Mrs Flowers to discuss the case, for she had a plan that could solve it, but she would need help from Claire and Mrs Flowers, so before the meeting started, when they were having refreshments in Mrs Flowers' kitchen, Molly had an announcement to make. "I am going to ask both of you for your help, and I shall pay you both for your time and effort from the money Mrs Curtis will give me when the case is solved." Claire looked at Mrs Flowers and Mrs Flowers looked at Claire both wondering which one of them was going to correct Molly. Claire gave Mrs Flowers a nod that she was the one to correct Molly for her silly notion that they would take money for helping out a friend. Mrs Flowers made a good job of it without hurting anyone's feelings.

The three of them had their meeting in Mrs Flowers' sitting room. Molly brought them up to date on the case and told them how she had seen Juliet's house. "It is a detached house with a high wall all around the garden," said Molly. "There is an old stable in the back garden that can be seen through a wire meshed fence which separates the back garden from the garden at the front of the house. At the back of the houses on Juliet's side of the street are public playing fields. Now the strange thing is that when Juliet came home from work in her car, she went into the house and then went straight way into the stable, and back out after a minute or so. Why do you think she did that?" asked Molly.

Claire did not answer right away, but said nothing and waited for Mrs Flowers' response, for she wanted Mrs Flowers to feel part of the team and not someone who had no say in the matter. Mrs Flowers thought hard and then answered. "I think she is checking up on something. I think she has hidden the letters in the stable and wants to make sure they are still there." Mrs Flowers had become rather excited having worked out why Juliet had gone into the stable. "I myself often check up on things, such as have I switched off the cooker before I go shopping, or did I put the milk back in the fridge? I think Juliet must have been worried that the letters could have been stolen if left in the house, so she has hidden them somewhere in the old stable. Why else should she go there as soon as she returns home?" Mrs Flowers then jumped out of her seat and looked at Claire and Molly who she hoped would back her theory.

"I think *you* are right, Mrs Flowers," said Molly.

"What do you think, Claire?"

"I agree with Mrs Flowers."

"I think we should all go tomorrow and see if she does the same thing again when she comes home after work," said Mrs Flowers. They all thought that was a good idea, and agreed to go the next day.

"As we all think she will go into the stable to check up on the letters, then tomorrow I want to find out what she does when she is in the stable," said Molly. I propose to be in the stable when she enters. I could go into the stable and hide, say twenty minutes before she returns home

"But you have told us, Molly, that there is a high wall around the garden. How will you get over the wall and reach the stable?" asked Mrs Flowers.

"I was hoping Claire would give me a bunk-up over the wall," said Molly.

"I can do that," said Claire, "but when you come to the stable what will you do Molly, because you will find that it's locked?"

"I will unlock the stable door with my skeleton keys. It will probably be a bolt with a padlock. I will go into the stable and hide. Claire, you will have to lock the stable door, then hide in the garden. When Juliet returns from work, she will go to the stable, unlock the door and enter to check that her letters are still there. When she leaves she will lock the door,so Claire you then have to unlock the door so I can get back out."

"I think it is a splendid plan, Molly," said Claire.

"However, I do think I should be the one to go into the stable to hide, and let you do all the locking and opening of the stable door. You are the expert at that, and I would feel uneasy at having to use the skeleton key. If I can't get it to work, you may be locked up in the stable all night long."

"I think Claire is right, Molly. You really should be in charge of the lock, as you are the expert," said Mrs Flowers. Molly just had to agree.

They then discussed in greater detail what had to be done. Claire was the first to speak. "We will need a thick rope to get over the wall plus a thick blanket and two pairs of garden gloves in case there is glass on the top of the wall."

"You will probably find all that in my garden shed," said Mrs Flowers. It was agreed that they were to communicate by their phones and had to make sure no sound came from them when they were over the wall.

"I will have to meet you tomorrow morning before school," said Molly "We will practise wall climbing by using Mrs Flowers' wall, and we will need that thick rope."

"I can assure you there is one in the garden shed," said Mrs Flowers.

CHAPTER 35
The Plan Starts

When Claire came home from school the next day she changed into her everyday clothes. She was soon on her way with Molly, Mrs Flowers, Big Dog and Mitzy heading for the playing fields behind Juliet's house. Mrs Flowers drove them all to the road at the side of the playing fields and parked in the car park. They all got out of the car and Claire handed her two dogs into the care of Mrs Flowers. "I'll walk Mitzy and Big Dog now along the street where Juliet's house is," said Mrs Flowers. Molly had taken photos of the house along with photos of Juliet and her car and had shown them to Mrs Flowers, so she was well prepared. "The moment I spot Juliet, I'll let you both know. Good luck in climbing over the wall at Juliet's back garden. I'm sure you will manage it." Mrs Flowers then departed with the dogs while Molly and Claire, each carrying a large bag containing things they may need, entered the playing fields.

The playing fields were not fenced off in any way, so Molly and Claire just walked at the side of the field next to the walls of the back gardens until they came to the back of Juliet's house. They looked around and found the playing fields were almost deserted except for a few boys kicking a ball about at the far end, and who were paying no attention to their presence. Molly and Claire then looked up at the wall to find it was much higher than the one they had practised on that morning.

Molly began to despair, but Claire was confident they both would conquer the wall. There appeared to be no glass cemented to the top of the wall, but the wall was very old and there may yet be a remnant. The wall stretched for quite a distance giving Claire a good choice of the spot where she could attack it. She picked the spot behind a tall bush in the garden. She put on her gloves as did Molly, looked around to see all was clear, then threw the blanket up on the wall so it covered the top. She bent her knees then leapt up into the air and grabbed hold of the other side of the wall. Molly looked on in amazement for she knew that she could never have done that. Claire pulled herself up and sat on the wall.

She had been right, there had been glass on the wall, but most had broken off by now with just little bits here and there. Molly threw the rope up to Claire, who then pulled Molly up so that both now sat on the wall. Claire then lowered Molly to the ground on the other side of the wall using the rope, and then holding on to the other side of the wall, lowered herself down, let go and joined her. The two friends then ran to the stable where Molly, using her skeleton keys, found one that worked, letting her open the large padlock. "You are really good at that, Molly," said Claire, who this time was the one standing watching her in amazement. Claire could have probably opened the padlock too, but in a much longer time.

Claire entered the stable alone, while Molly closed the stable door so that Claire was now well and truly locked up all alone in the stable. Molly then hid in the garden and waited. Claire, alone in the stable, climbed a rickety ladder and landed up in the loft where she now waited. Both Claire and Molly contacted Mrs Flowers' to tell her they were in position.

Mrs Flowers now had an important job to do as she walked Mitzy and Big Dog along the street where Juliet lived, while at the same time looking out for the arrival of Juliet in her white car. Juliet arrived at the time predicted by Molly, and parked, not in front of the porch as she had done the day before, but this time at the side of the road opposite her house. Mrs Flowers contacted Claire and Molly to put them on red alert. Both muted their phones. The big question now was, would Juliet go to the stable and do whatever she did there.

They were not held in suspense very long, for Juliet did emerge from the back door and headed for the stable. Molly watched her from her hiding place in the garden as Juliet undid the padlock and entered the stable. Claire heard the door creek open as the stable was flooded with light.

CHAPTER 36
The Metal Box

Juliet went over to the food trough which was full of straw, thrust her hand into it and extracted a metal box. She opened the box, looked inside, closed it and returned it to its hiding place. She left happy, for she liked to make sure her hidden treasure was still there in its place, and was as safe as houses. A few minutes later Molly sent Claire a text saying Juliet was back in her house. Claire came down from the loft, found the box and opened it. She smiled when she saw the bundle of letters which had caused such trouble. The letters were tied up with a thin red ribbon. She removed them from the box and was surprised when she discovered another bundle of letters tied with a thin blue ribbon. She left them in the box while she flicked through the red ribbon letters, and found there were indeed eleven of them as she had been told. She then removed the remaining letters from the metal box and examined them. She saw at a glance that they were written by the same hand, on the same type of paper with the same ink. She placed the letters into her backpack and then added the blue bundle, having removed the blue and red ribbons.

She had found what she had come for, plus a bonus bundle, and now it was time to leave, but not before doing one more thing. She toppled over the feeding trough and left the metal box open on its side among the straw on the ground. From her backpack she took out a paper bag containing the torn bits of letter paper that Molly and Mrs Flowers had prepared the night before. She sprinkled the torn paper around the metal container and in other places in the stable. She then added the blue and red ribbons to the torn paper. Claire had done a good job for it did look as if mice had nibbled away at the letters.

She then texted Molly to come and unlock the stable door. Molly emerged from her hiding place and opened the padlock, which now let Claire push open the door and emerge from the stable. She gave the thumbs up to Molly who then shut the door and locked the padlock. They now had to leave the garden without being seen by Juliet who was in the house. They ran along the side wall to the back wall of the garden where they were hidden from view from the house by the large bush. Soon they were over the wall and back in the car park where sitting waiting for them in her car was Mrs Flowers and the dogs.

"We got the letters," cried Molly, as they entered

the car.

"How did you get on, Mrs Flowers?" asked Claire.

"It went like clockwork. Juliet arrived on time, but the funny thing is she just parked in the street outside her house. I think she is going out again, maybe for a weekend stay somewhere."

"Do you think you could please drive to the street where Juliet's house is, Mrs Flowers, and park where we can watch her car from a distance?" asked Molly.

"Certainly," said Mrs Flowers, as she started to drive off, "but do tell me, why are we going there?"

"I want to see if your hunch is right, that she is going away somewhere for the weekend."

"What I have heard of her I would not be surprised," said Mrs Flowers.

It did not take long to prove that Mrs Flowers had indeed been right, for just after a short time of surveillance, out came Juliet carrying an overnight bag which she put on the passenger seat of her car and then drove off. "I'm glad we saw that," said |Mrs Flowers. "That should make our phoney mice nibbling bits of paper look more plausible. I think the next time she visits her house will be on Monday after work. She is going to get one big surprise when she goes to the stable." They then headed for home.

When they arrived at Mrs Flowers' house Claire handed Molly the bundle of eleven letters and the extra bundle to a very surprised Mrs Flowers. Claire left, and was soon back home helping out in the kitchen. Molly and Mrs Flowers went to the sitting room where they looked at all the letters until dinner was to be served.

CHAPTER 37
The Letters

After dinner Mrs Flowers and Molly went to the sitting room to discuss what had to be done next. Mrs Flowers read every letter thoroughly for she thought it was the wise thing to do. "No wonder they wanted them back, Molly," said Mrs Flowers. "Mrs Curtis told me she was willing to pay a detective two hundred thousand pounds to get her hands on them. She has plenty of money, so I am going to help you make up the bill you will give her. I have to get paid for my part I played and so has Claire, although we will not be taking any of the money she hands over. I shall write out the bill now, and I shall phone Mrs Curtis to let her know we will visit her tomorrow morning to discuss the case. We will not tell her about the extra letters until you get paid, Molly."

When they arrived the next morning at Mrs Curtis' mansion they just went into the kitchen and sat around the kitchen table. "How is the case going, Molly?" asked Mrs Curtis. "Have you given up or do you just want to keep trying to solve it? Don't worry if you want to quit, for I am beginning to think an older detective may be a better bet. You mustn't feel it is your fault, Molly," and she went rabbiting on and on for several more minutes.

Molly said not a word, but reached into her briefcase and brought out the eleven letters. Mrs Curtis could hardly believe it was true when Molly told her the letters were the eleven letters that she had asked Molly to find. "I just don't believe you," snapped Mrs Curtis, and tried to grab the letters out of Molly's hand but failed.

"Pick a letter between one and eleven," Molly told Mrs Curtis.

"I pick number one," said Mrs Curtis, annoyed that a young girl was telling her to do something. Mrs Curtis read the letter and was flabbergasted.

"Is it genuine?" asked Molly

"It is genuine", she muttered. "Where did you get hold of it?" Molly did not answer her question, but chose rather to hand her the bill for the work that had been done in finding the letters.

"What is this?" asked Mrs Curtis.

"It's the bill for finding the letters. I don't accept cheques." Mrs Curtis looked at it.

"What!" she cried, when her eyes nearly popped out of their sockets when she saw the amount of money Molly was asking. "You are just a young girl and that is far too much money to ask for. You had better think again, my child. Anyway, how do I know if the other letters are genuine? And besides you have not told me where you got the letters from."

"Just hand that letter back and I shall give you another letter to see if you think it is authentic," said Molly, who held up the letters in front of her face. Mrs Curtis tried to grab them again, but failed. "Which letter would you like?" asked Molly, as she flicked through them numbering as she went.

"Number nine," snarled Mrs Curtis, who reluctantly handed back the letter she had just authenticated, and grabbed letter nine from Molly's hand. She read it and found it was indeed genuine. She was still reluctant to admit that a young girl like Molly had found and returned the letters. Just a day ago she was all for Molly, but that night she seemed to flip and regretted that she had ever set eyes on her.

"Well," said Mrs Flowers, "are you going to validate that letter also?"

"Yes, I suppose so," said Mrs Curtis reluctantly, "but I still think she is asking too much money for a couple of days' work. Mrs Curtis had now changed her reason for not wanting to pay the bill.

"The blackmailer was asking one hundred times more than what Molly is asking," said Mrs Flowers, who decided it was time to step up and support Molly. "I think you have been offered a good deal, and besides, Molly has put herself in great danger getting these letters for you."

"Very well," said a very angry Mrs Curtis, and went

to collect her cheque book from the escritoire in the room. As she did so Molly retrieved the letter she had given Mrs Curtis and added it to her bundle.

"Please make the cheque payable to me, Mrs Curtis," requested Mrs Flowers, for that is what Molly wants." Molly had indeed asked Mrs Flowers to request this as she had no bank account. "You will get the letters handed over when this cheque clears," said Mrs Flowers, as she got up and left along with Molly and the letters.

They were soon back in Mrs Flowers' sitting room where Molly thanked Mrs Flowers for her help in negotiating the bill. Molly went into her briefcase and took out both bundles of letters. "I was planning to give the extra bundle to Mrs Curtis after the cheque is cleared, but because of her appalling behaviour I changed my mind and wanted to ask you what I should do with them now."

"Goodness Molly! That was a very smart move of yours. I'm glad you kept it a secret from her," said Mrs Flowers. "Would you like to keep them in my safe?"

"Oh, yes please," replied Molly.

"I think we will be hearing from Mrs Curtis again quite soon," said Mrs Flowers with a big smile, and then we can work out what to do with the extra bundle."

Joe then came to collect Molly and she was soon back home.

CHAPTER 38
No Charge

Now Juliet had been away from her home for three nights and returned on Monday just after six pm. When she looked into the stable, as was her habit, she gave out a despairing cry of horror which must have been heard a good distance away. She fell for the deception that some animal, probably a fox, had overturned the feeding trough causing the metal box to open and the letters fall out which were destroyed by mice.

It was not until Wednesday that Juliet again phoned Mrs Curtis demanding she pay her for the letters and not only that, for she went on to tell Mrs Curtis she had more compromising letters, which Mrs Curtis could have along with the others for double the price. Mrs Curtis got on the phone straight away and asked Mrs Flowers for a meeting with Molly. Molly was back home but agreed to take a phone call from Mrs Curtis, on one of her phones. Mrs Curtis told Molly about the phone call from Juliet. "I'll meet you on Saturday at noon at Mrs Flowers' house," Molly told her and ended the phone call.

On Saturday morning Joe arrived with Molly and the children, allowing Molly and the children to play in the garden for most of the morning, while Joe worked on his car. Just before noon Mrs Flowers phoned Mrs Curtis to come and collect the extra bundle of letters. She arrived in her car just as fast as she could, with her cheque book in her hand. She was shown into the sitting room where Mrs Flowers and Molly were. Molly handed her the eleven letters plus the extra ones, and asked her to verify their authenticity which she did. "How much do I owe you?" asked Mrs Curtis, who opened her cheque book as she stood in front of Molly with pen in hand.

"How much do you owe me, Mrs Curtis? Nothing," said Molly, who turned on her heels and left, closing the door behind her. Molly went into the taxi and Joe drove off, with Molly and the children, watched by Mrs Flowers and Mrs Curtis through the sitting room window. Not knowing quite what to say Mrs Curtis then left for home.

It was now time for lunch and they all went to the dinning room where Claire had been waiting for them, and of course the children were delighted to meet Claire again. It all had been arranged by Molly, Claire and Mrs Flowers. After lunch Claire went back to her own kitchen and Joe put all their things in his car. "Let's go and see Mrs Low," said Molly. They went into Joe's car and Mrs Flowers waved them goodbye.

CHAPTER 39

The Birthday Girl

Joe drove the short distance to Mrs Goodyard's mansion where Claire and the staff were waiting for them. Now Claire knew all the children's birthdays, and it just so happened that that very day was Gemma's birthday. Claire had baked Gemma a very nice birthday cake and had decorated it with icing, using her own money to buy all the ingredients.

All those working in the kitchen also knew it was Gemma's birthday and that Joe had come to take Molly and the children home. It was no surprise to them when they heard that special, familiar knock at the kitchen door. Claire went to a cupboard to collect the cake and place it on the kitchen table, but she was suddenly struck with a rather disturbing feeling of guilt. "What am I doing?" she asked herself. "Gemma's mum will have bought or made her a cake, besides looking after the rest of the children. How would I like it if I had made a cake for my child and someone came along with a much better cake? I would not like that at all and neither would Gemma's mum. No, I should never have made the cake in the first place." Claire left the cake sitting in the cupboard. The staff had been waiting to open the door once the cake was on the table. They all understood why Claire had done what she had just done.

The knocking sounded again. "Is that the birthday girl and Tommy?" enquired Mrs Low.

"Yes it is," answered a small excited voice.

"Do come in." They entered along with Molly and their brother Joe.

"How did you know it was my birthday, Mrs Low?" asked Gemma. Mrs Low said not a word, but simply tapped twice the side of her nose with her index finger and smiled.

"The four of you come and sit down at the table before you go, and have something to eat and drink," said Claire's mum.

"How old are you then?" asked Bella.

"Five."

"And you Tommy?"

"Three and a half." It was then Tommy returned Mrs Low's custard jar. As they were all chatting, Ms Low went to the cupboard and handed Gemma a birthday card from all of them.

"Thank you," said Gemma, and gave Mrs Low a thank you hug. It was soon time to leave and Joe thanked everyone for their kindness.

"I'm glad this time it was a birthday card and not a jar full of custard along with tarts," said Molly.

"We don't want you to think we just come here to say goodbye so we get custard and tarts, but we do come to say goodbye because we are going to miss you all. Aren't we, children?" asked Molly. They all agreed.

"But before you leave," said Claire's mum, Mrs Low has something to say.

Mrs Low bent down and produced from a box under the table a custard jar full of custard. "I just want to say, don't forget the jar next time you call." They all laughed. A bunch of apple and blackberry tarts were also produced, and they all helped carry them to Joe's taxi. They waved goodbye as they drove off and went back to the kitchen, each with the sense of loneliness in their hearts, as they got back to work.

"I wish we could have bought some toys for Gemma, but it wouldn't be fair, I suppose," said Bella

"I know," said Mrs Low, "for if our toys had been better than the ones Gemma's mother had got for her, then that would have been just awful!"

"You did well, Claire," said her mum. "Sometimes it is better to let someone find out for themselves than having to tell them they are going down the wrong path." Claire then went to see Mrs Flowers and thanked her for her part in setting up the surprise party.

CHAPTER 40
Helping a Stranger

One day Claire was making her way alone across the playground when she spotted an older girl who ran and caught up with her. "Excuse me," called out the girl, "are you Claire?"

"Yes, I am," answered Claire. "Can I help you?"

"I'm Angela, I was wondering if I could talk to you alone for a few minutes. I have been asking around and have learned that you have been known to help others."

They went over to a quiet part of the playground where Angela told her story to Claire. "All my life I have attended a boarding school, but when my father's business collapsed just a month ago, he went bankrupt and could no longer pay the school fees, so here I am in the senior form at your school. I had only been here for a few days when the bullying started by a group of girls in my year group, led by a girl called Kitty. They say I have no business being in this school and I should go back to my boarding school, post haste. I have no intention of giving into their demands."

"Nor should you," remarked Claire. "I have heard bad things about Kitty. She always seems to pick on anyone who is rather nice and not looking for confrontation. However, I can see you are made of sterner stuff, Angela.

"I was wondering if you could give me advice on how to handle bullying in this school. It may be entirely different from the way they handled it in my old school, so I just don't want to make a fool of myself."

"What I do know is the top management of the school will be on Kitty's side," said Claire with regret. They will regard you as a loser and not worth listening to. Also Kitty's father is on the school's Parents Teacher Association which helps Kitty's case. I'll need to do some research on this and then we can discuss what has to be done. Would you like to join me and my friends at our table for lunch, Angela?" asked Claire.

"Very much," said Angela. "It shall be a change at having to sit alone in the canteen. Kitty makes sure that I do so." At the table Claire introduced Angela to her friends. It was Eleanor's turn that day to say grace, but with her eyes, she let Claire know she could say grace if she chose. Claire indeed accepted Eleanor's invitation and after thanking God for the food they were about to enjoy, asked that all present would be under His protection

As she ate Claire would look over at Kitty's table, and found that Kitty was keeping an eye on both herself and Angela. To Claire, Kitty looked angry, very angry indeed. "It's soon going to be showdown time," said Claire to herself.

When Kitty and her gang left, Claire took note as did the others sitting with her. A minute later, Claire left her table saying she had something to do and would be back shortly. Eleanor and Rosie looked at each other with concern for Claire's safety. As Claire left the canteen and entered the playground she slowly headed for the main building. She was now being approached by Kitty who felt the time was ripe to put Claire well and truly in her proper place.

Kitty came right up to Claire, stood in front of her and blocked her progress. "I want to talk to you, but not here in the middle of the playground," she told Claire, in no uncertain terms. "If you are not as stupid as you look, you will come with me where we can have a private conversation."

"Where are we going?" asked Claire, as Kitty grabbed Claire by the arm.

"Where are we going? We are going behind the gym. It's private there." Claire let Kitty drag her along, for she did not want Kitty to know that she was actually hoping that that would be their destination. Claire was not in awe of Kitty or feared her at all, but nevertheless was careful.

As they disappeared behind the gym and along the path at the side of the gym, Claire shook off Kitty's grip and put a one metre distance between herself and Kitty as they walked side by side. "This is as far as we go," said Kitty. Claire suddenly heard voices behind her and turned round to see a group of Kitty's friends enter the pathway behind the gym.

"Well, what do you want to tell me?" asked Claire, while still keeping a safe distance from Kitty.

"Here's what you do. You keep away from Angela and completely ignore her," growled Kitty.

"And if I don't?" asked Claire.

"You have no choice. You'll do as I tell you, you little brat."

"I have no intention of doing what you want," said Claire defiantly, as she stood there hands on hips and a big smile on her face as she looked up at Kitty. That was too much for Kitty. She had never in all her life met such defiance. She sprang at Claire with fists flying in the air. She missed, and missed again and again. She took a rest and then had one more go. She hurled herself at Claire in a rugby tackle, but found nothing to grab onto and landed face down on the ground. "I'm off now," said Claire. "Would you like me to help you up before I go?" That really annoyed Kitty, so she got to her feet and looked around. Her gang, which had just witnessed her humiliation, were standing close by staring at her. They had come to enjoy watching their leader humiliating Claire, but this time it was their leader who had been humiliated.

"Grab her," yelled Kitty, while pointing her finger at Claire. They simply shook their heads, turned and made their way along the path and were back in the playground. They no longer wanted a loser like Kitty as their gang leader. They had seen the real Kitty for the first time and they just did not like the view, for they had now realised that she was just another pathetic bully

"Well that's that done," said Claire, as she sat down and joined her friends. "How long was I away for?"

Jennifer looked at her watch. "Just over ten minutes." Rosie and Eleanor smiled at each other for they had a good idea of what Claire had been up to.

CHAPTER 41

Kitty's Revenge

It was the next morning when things began to flare up. The school bus that Claire was on drew up in the car park just opposite the school and the children started getting out. When Claire was going down the steps to get off the bus, it all began. A person, dressed in overalls and wearing a mask, approached the bus and then suddenly from behind their back produced a bucket filled with some kind of liquid. The liquid was then thrown at Claire as she stepped down from the bus, however she was too quick to be caught out and dived to her left landing safely on the ground. As Claire was no longer there to stop the liquid it landed on the person directly behind Claire and soaked him with what looked like a purple dye. His name was Darrell and from his stomach down to his feet he was covered in purple dye. If it had landed on Claire it would have landed on her face which could have caused serious injuries.

The boy just stood there on the steps of the bus trying to work out just what had happened, but Claire had got to her feet and was chasing the culprit. The perpetrator of the crime had an accomplice who had been parked in a car as near to the bus as possible. The driver of the car opened the passenger door and the masked thrower got in and away they went. Just a few seconds later a school boy on a bicycle came by heading for the school. Claire ran up to him and blocked his passage. "It's an emergency," cried Claire. "I need to borrow your bike," but he was reluctant to do so.

"Just give her the bike. It is an emergency," shouted someone in the small crowd that had come from the bus. He complied and in no time at all Claire was in hot pursuit of the car. She could see the car in the distance as the road was straight before coming to a bend. When the car disappeared round the bend Claire was not that far behind for her pedalling power was remarkable.

On turning round the bend Claire got quite a surprise, for there was the car only a few hundred metres in front of her. She stopped immediately and backed into the bend at a place where she could watch the car and not be seen. She took out her phone and started to record what was happening. The doors of the car were being opened, and out came Kitty and the driver. Kitty was holding the bucket that had been used in the attack and threw it into the ditch at the side of the road. The driver then went to the front of the car and Kitty to the back where she bent down next to the car's licence plate. It turned out to be a fake one clipped onto the original plate. Kitty removed the fake licence plate, revealing the original one.

Claire had captured it all on her phone, and now it was time to get back to the bus. Soon she was back and returned the bike to Darrell who had changed into his gym kit.

"I shall have to be off now," said the bus driver. "I think you should report the incident to your headteacher."

CHAPTER 42
A Deal is Reached.

Just as the bus was leaving Kitty's car drove into the car park and Kitty got out dressed in her usual school outfit. As the bus driver left he gave them a toot, and the crowd all gave him a wave. Kitty gave him the biggest wave of all trying to draw as much attention to herself as she could.

A gym teacher, who was heading for the school's car park, stopped his car and went over to the group of children which by now had grown somewhat larger. "Why is this boy in his gym kit?" he asked.

Darrell explained what had happened. Meanwhile Kitty, who had been watching the group, walked over and joined them. She wanted to show to the teacher that she had just arrived and thought this was a great opportunity to establish her alibi. What has been going on?" she asked in her most innocent of voices. "I have just arrived." While she was talking Claire approached her, and looked her up and down, which made Kitty feel very uncomfortable. Claire had found not one spot of purple dye on Kitty's school clothing.

"You have missed a drop," said Claire, as she looked Kitty in the eye.

"Whatever are you talking about, girl?" she snarled.

"Your shoes, there are splashes of purple dye on them. You should have been more careful when you removed your overalls and mask. Don't you agree?" Kitty looked down at her shoes and just stared at them for a moment while she was trying to think of some explanation she could give for the purple stains.

"Someone must have flicked it on my shoes by mistake," she stammered, hoping that they would accept her explanation.

Unfortunately for Kitty, no one believed her feeble excuse, but just stood and stared at her. "What are you all staring at?" she screamed. "I had nothing to do with the boy being drenched. In fact, I don't even know his name." Kitty was panicking trying to prove her innocence. "So there is purple dye on my shoes. Someone has flicked it on them by mistake. Look, there is no purple dye on my hands." She held up her hands for all to see. As she did so the sleeves of her jacket slipped down her arms just a few inches, but nevertheless revealed her wrists with traces of purple dye.

"That must have got there when she was removing her dye stained vinyl gloves," said Darrell "It was you, Kitty, who soaked me with that purple dye."

Here the teacher intervened. "Darrell, you report to the school office at nine o'clock and you too Kitty."

They did report and Mr Neal looked into the case. The evidence against Kitty was overwhelming, so Kitty had to admit that she was guilty of soaking the boy. However, Kitty played the victim and said that she had been told that a boy had been calling her names, and it was just a warning to him to stop. She admitted she got the wrong boy, was very sorry and would never do anything like that again.

Finally, just to show how nice she really was, she said she would use her pocket money to buy Darrell a new set of clothes. Mr Neal thought that was a good settlement and persuaded Darrell to think that too. So that brought an end to it all, and of course nothing was done about Claire almost being blinded.

When Claire got home that day she printed out photos of the changing of the licence plates. Next day Kitty came up to Claire with a big smirk all over her face. "Hard luck, better luck next time little girl. You are just not smart enough to get me into any trouble."

"Really!" said Claire, and showed her a photo of her changing the licence plate with her brother in the background with a fake plate in his hand.

"You leave me and Angela alone from now on. If I hear of you causing any trouble to anyone at all, then this picture and the others will be sent to the police and the licensing authority. Kitty's smirk had gone and she left with her face looking a shade paler. The result was that the two girls never had any more trouble from that bully, and by the way, Darrell never got a new set of clothes.

CHAPTER 43
Envy

Some people don't like seeing others doing well and there was a good example of this in Claire's maths class. It was the top maths class for Claire's year group and Claire had landed in it because she had done extraordinarily well in an inter school maths competition. Olive, a hard working girl in the class, would always get top marks in tests and exams for maths and this annoyed Len, who thought he should always be top of the class. Whenever the opportunity arose he would do his best to degrade Olive. If they passed each other in the corridor he would show his disgust for her by uttering a disparaging word as they passed by and then make a sort of spitting noise. Claire had seen him do just that several times in the corridor and he even tried it in the maths class, but the teacher Miss Millard soon put a stop to that. It was then Claire decided to act the next time Len would step out of line.

In the canteen Len had now started to deliberately bump into Olive. Now was the time for Claire to act. She would make sure she was always close to Olive in the canteen queue and when they were walking to their tables. Olive hardly ever noticed the presence of Claire and that could be said about Len also, who was always looking for an opportunity to humiliate Olive. One day Olive was setting off for her table, with a cup of juice sitting next to her meal on her tray, which to Len's eyes made it look irresistible. It should be remembered he was filled with hatred just because she got better marks than he did. He was being stupid letting such a thing annoy him, and now he was about to do a rather stupid thing. Dislike of Olive had turned to hate, and hate most times ends up with the hate filled person doing some really absurd acts when trying to destroy the person they hate.

Len, who was following Olive, had a big grin on his face picturing the havoc he thought he was about to cause. His grin grew bigger and bigger the closer he got to Olive. Little did he know that Claire was just behind him. Suddenly Len tried to strike Olive's shoulder so that she would drop the tray, making it look like it was her fault. The only thing that went wrong with his plan was that he had not taken into account the presence of Claire. Instead of striking the back of Olive's shoulder and knocking the tray out of her hands, his hand was gripped by Claire's free hand and pulled down to his side. The hapless boy cried out with shock as his tray dropped to the floor with a clatter. Claire, nimble as ever, had taken a step back, and when all eyes in the canteen turned to see what had caused the racket, they only saw Olive standing there with her tray safely in her hands with Len behind her with a dazed look on his face, while his tray, with its contents lay scattered on the floor.

CHAPTER 44
The Test

From that day forth Len stopped his physical attacks on Olive, but increased his verbal threats on her. He was now looking for an opportunity when he could physically harm Claire. To her surprise Claire noticed a distinctive change for the worse in Olive's appearance and her work. Claire so far had never spoken to Olive, but now she felt compelled to do so in order to find out what exactly was happening to her. One day when they were both alone Claire approached her. "How are you keeping, Olive?" asked Claire.

Olive was surprised at Claire asking the question, and just gave the usual answer that she was fine. "Why do you ask, Claire?"

"Because you have not been looking like yourself recently," said Claire, and paused to see if Olive in some way would respond, but she said not a word. So Claire just asked bluntly. "Are you being bullied or threatened by Len?"

"Yes, I am, Claire," she answered almost immediately, for now she would be able to talk to someone at last who seemed to care about the abuse she had to put up with from Len. She then told Claire about how she had been threatened by Len and what the consequences would be if she ever again got better marks than he did. "As you know Claire, we are getting a test this Wednesday and getting it back on Friday. I just don't know what to do."

"Just go ahead as usual, Olive," said Claire. "I am now going to give him someone else to worry about rather than you."

"And who will that be?" asked Olive

"Why, my very self," said Claire and smiled.

It was during the last period on Friday when the results of the maths' test were handed out. The first pupil to be given back their test paper was a boy who got sixty four percent. Now that would have been a good mark in most classes, but this was the top Maths class and more was expected from them. It did not take long to hand back the papers and give out the marks. Soon there were only three more papers to hand back. Miss Millard, as was her custom, would withhold the three best marks to the end and hand them back in no particular order.

The first paper was handed to Len who was all smiles, thinking he was top of the class, but when Olive's name was read out with a better score the smile quickly disappeared to be replaced by a scowl on his sallow face. Yet there was still another paper to be handed back with one hundred percent written in bold red letters next to the name of Claire. "And finally the top mark goes to Claire," announced Miss Millard, as she handed Claire her paper. "You all did very well, and it is time to go over the exam paper to see your mistakes." Poor Len, he just sat at his desk now with a blank look on his face. What had gone wrong and how on earth had Claire suddenly obtained the top mark was all that was on his mind. All thoughts of Olive had vanished and had been replaced by Claire, and how he would sort her out.. That night he worked out a plan of what must be done and he could hardly wait to carry it out.

CHAPTER 45
Len introduced Himself

Next day at lunchtime Len approached Claire as she was crossing the playground heading for the canteen. "I was wondering if I could talk to you about the Maths Class?" he asked Claire.

"Certainly, Len," said Claire.

"It's rather confidential," he said, "so let's go to a quiet part of the playground." When they got there he started his rant. "I don't want you ever again to beat me in a Maths test and that will apply to your so-called friend Olive, so you give her the message."

"Certainly not," said Claire emphatically.

"You certainly will or it will be the worst for you," threatened Len, as he rushed at her with his fists flying here, there and everywhere. Claire easily dogged his vicious blows and let him just go on and on in his vain attempts to hurt her. He continued until he had no strength left, and fell to his knees exhausted. There he crouched, head in his hands when suddenly he gave out a cry of frustration and lay face down on the ground, and with the little energy he had left started pounding the ground with his fists.

No one in the playground could see him, for he had chosen a spot to confront Claire hidden by part of the school building. It was time now for Claire to act. She got him to his feet and then taking him by the arm they sat down on an empty bench. "Why did you want to hurt me, Len?" asked Claire. There was silence and just when Claire thought he was not going to answer he began to sound off.

"Why, you ask," he roared. "Why? I just do." He stopped talking and turned and looked Claire right in the eyes. Claire gave him a searching glance, eager to know his answer. He looked at Claire and for the first time saw her as a human being

"Is it because I beat you in a test?" asked Claire. He did not answer, but turned away from Claire and looked at the ground. He seemed to be thinking, and was slowly calming down. He looked at Claire again, and then for some reason or other he started to tell the truth.

"I just have to win. I just have to get the school prize in as many subjects as possible. I have to study every night and every day of the week. My father wants me to be a doctor just like his nephew. Father has not been keeping well lately and I did not want to upset him by not getting top marks. I must get the school prize for Maths."

"Let's be friends instead of enemies," suggested Claire. "Shall we go to the canteen and have lunch together? Come and sit with my group of friends.

Shall we go?" Len nodded and they headed for the canteen. There they collected their meal and Claire took Len to her table and introduced him to her friends.

"Oh, I know Len already," said Eleanor, when Claire introduced him. "He is in our English class. He always gets top marks." Rosie said grace and hoped they all would become good friends.

For the rest of the week Len joined Claire's table for lunch. On Friday Claire invited him to join them at the Sunday School on Sunday afternoon. "I would like to, but I shall have to ask my father. I shall phone you tonight if he gives me permission to attend." Claire never received the phone call so Len never turned up.

"Are you keeping well, Len?" Claire asked him, when they sat down for lunch at their usual table. Only Jennifer had arrived so Claire thought it may be an opportune moment to ask him some personal questions.

"I am, but my father was taken to hospital in an ambulance last night, and I'm dreadfully worried. Mother has almost had a breakdown, and just sits around and mopes."

"Can we help you in any way?"

"We will soon be running out of food if Mum does not snap out of it. I don't know what we will do as Dad holds the purse strings."

"Give us a list of things you usually buy and we shall try and get them for you," suggested Claire.

"How are you going to do that, Claire?" asked Jennifer.

"Mrs Flowers will help."

Mrs Flowers indeed helped. With the list from Len, and along with Jennifer and Claire, Mrs Flowers bought and supplied whatever was required. They helped in the kitchen until Len's mother once again could manage on her own. Len's father was less than a week in hospital and then a couple of weeks in the house before returning to work. When again Len asked his father if he could go to Sunday School with Mrs Flowers and her helpers, to his great surprise his father granted his request.

CHAPTER 46

Claire the Gymnast

Now Claire used to be in a gymnastics club in a previous school and she often longed to try out some of her skills. She knew the school she was now attending had set up a gymnastics club and decided to see if she could join, so one day after a gym lesson she stayed behind at the morning break and asked the teacher, Miss Dexter, if she could join. Miss Dexter asked Claire if she could perform a few basic gymnastics moves to which Claire replied she could. She then asked Claire if she could do certain floor exercises and if she could perform on the beam. Claire again said she could. Miss Dexter doubted it very much and had just asked to find out if Claire had been telling the truth.

"I want you, Claire, to come down to the gym hall tomorrow at the morning interval and let me see you perform. The equipment will be already set up, for the senior pupils will have been using it. I expect to see you tomorrow morning, and remember to bring your costume." Claire thanked Miss Dexter and left. She knew that Miss Dexter thought she was not telling the truth, and tomorrow was just a test to see if she was a liar or not.

Next day at the morning interval Claire called in at the gym hall and knocked at the staff door. It was opened by Miss Dexter who could not disguise her surprise to see Claire standing there alone.

"I thought she would be absent from school today, but now she is going to tell me she has sprained her ankle or some other lie," thought Miss Dexter, as she stared down at Claire.

"I have brought my costume with me. Shall I change into it and go to the gym hall, Miss Dexter?" asked Claire.

"Yes," said Miss Dexter, slightly shocked at Claire's question.

A few minutes later found Claire and Miss Dexter alone in the hall, with Claire looking the part of a gymnast in her smart looking costume which she had altered slightly as she had grown since last using it. The mat was still there from the last lesson spread out over the floor. Miss Dexter then asked Claire to perform certain basic moves which she did perfectly. She then asked Claire to do the rather difficult floor move which Claire had claimed she could perform. "I shall try my best, Miss Dexter, but it has been quite a while since I last performed this move."

"Here we go, excuses, excuses," said Miss Dexter to herself. "I knew she could never do it." Oh how wrong could she be. Claire positioned herself at the edge of the mat, started her run and did two full rotations and landed at the other side of the mat.

"Shall I do the beam now, Miss?" asked Claire. Miss Dexter, lost for words, just nodded. Claire got onto the beam and performed a backflip with a full twist, landing back on the beam. She then came over to Miss Dexter to learn what she had thought of her performance. Will I be able to join the club?" asked Claire.

"Of course you may join. You better run along and get changed so you are not late for your next class." Claire left, and Miss Dexter returned to the teachers' staff room still amazed at what she had witnessed.

CHAPTER 47
Nice try Nancy

On Wednesday after school Claire did attend the club for the first time. She met with a sour look from some of the girls in the club, but most were indifferent about her presence, for they dreamed about winning medals and becoming famous, while Claire was there to keep fit and agile. Miss Dexter knew her girls well and knew if she asked Claire to perform certain moves that the rest of them could never really even think of doing, that it would just cause envy, so she just treated Claire like any other girl in the club. When it was time to go Claire thanked Miss Dexter for an enjoyable session and headed for the bus stop just outside the school.

Next day a girl came up to Claire in the playground. Claire knew her to be a member of the gymnastics club, and more importantly a friend of Nancy. "Hello, I'm Sally," she told Claire.

"Nice to meet you, Sally," said Claire. "I saw you perform yesterday. It looked very good."

"Why thank you, Claire. I'm sure if you work hard at it you may one day become just as good as I am."

"I do hope so, Sally," said Claire, who all the time was wondering what Sally was up to.

"We saw you standing waiting at the bus stop yesterday after the club had closed. Next time when the club meets we could give you a lift home in my brother's car when comes to collect us. Would you like that, Claire?"

"Very much," said Claire, most politely.

"It's a date then," said Sally, and left with a big grin on her face.

At the next weekly meeting of the club when they had just finished the session and were in the changing room, Sally and her two friends suddenly got up and left not having dressed properly. Claire noted it, quickly dressed and left having said goodbye to her teacher. She knew that they were up to no good and were probably going to drive off and abandon her.

When Claire got into the playground she was just in time to see Sally and her friends go into the car park close to the school gate, where her brother's car was parked. They did not get into the car, but just stood beside it no doubt waiting for Claire to arrive. It was then Claire noticed a girl sitting in the front passenger seat, and not to her surprise she recognised her as Nancy. "Well Nancy, I have been wondering when you were going to show up. Now I know," said Claire.

Claire went into her backpack, took out a greetings card and wrote a few words on it, and then put it into her pocket. She waited for a few minutes then walked towards the car. When they saw Claire approach Sally and her two friends waved to Claire, and then climbed into the car. When Claire reached the car, the passenger's window was lowered down and the face of Nancy appeared.

"Gotcha," cried Nancy. "Did you think anyone in this school would give you a lift home? If you did, you must be delusional." All eyes in the car were focused on the face of Claire who seemed to be very upset and about to burst into tears, as she stood all alone at the side of the car close to the windscreen. Nancy went on to end in a tirade of really harmful and nasty words.

While Nancy had been yapping away, Claire, unknown to the rest of them in the car, had placed the card that she had written just a few minutes ago, under a windscreen wiper. Having finished reviling Claire they drove off, but as they were about to exit the car park, the car suddenly stopped and out jumped Sally from the back seat and retrieved the card. "Read it out," cried Nancy, who could not wait to learn what was written. Sally humbly obeyed.

"Nice try Nancy, that is all it says."

"Let me see," cried Nancy, and snatched the card from the hand of Sally as she was handing it in through the window.

"How did the brat know I would be here," roared Nancy. "Who told her?" She ripped the card up, threw it on the ground, closed the window and they drove off again.

CHAPTER 48

The Competition

After the incident in the car park, Sally and her two friends in the gymnastics club did their best to ignore Claire, but Claire did not let that bother her at all. She just treated them as she treated anyone else in the club, with civility and respect. Miss Dexter, seeing how well Claire fitted in, asked her one day if she would like to be in the club's competition team. "Yes I would," answered Claire, "but just as a reserve. I would not like to replace anyone in the team."

"I shall keep you in mind then," said Miss Dexter. Claire, who had been in a competition once before, did not want to have to use her talents, but would use them only when the other side deserved to lose. Miss Dexter chose wisely when to pick Claire as one of the reserves. Her first contest was with a club that just happened to think they were the bee's knees and looked down on any other club that would oppose them.

The fixtures were held in the schools' gym halls, with away and home matches just like they do in a football league. The match Claire was in was a home one with the away event already having been played out with Claire's team winning narrowly, and receiving three points. The other team was looking for revenge and were well prepared for it by their new coach, Miss Law. It was to be judged by volunteers, most being elderly and retired former gymnastics teachers and performers.

The Saturday morning of the contest found Claire in the gym hall of her school waiting for the arrival of the opposition. When their bus arrived Miss Dexter went out to greet Miss Law and her team and showed them into the gym hall. Claire could hear them utter disparaging remarks about the hall and her team. The teams went to their dressing rooms and soon emerged ready to start. The judges were in place, the audience waited and the first part of the competition began. It was the floor exercises with the opposition easily in the lead. This caused Miss Law to confront Miss Dexter. "You should at least put up some show," said the angry Miss Law. "I get ever so embarrassed visiting schools like this one. I suggest you at least put in some effort to win and pick the girls in your team with some go about them."

Claire had heard every word issued by the high and mighty Miss Law and glanced over at her teacher, Miss Dexter. All Claire now did was to raise her eyebrow and give her head just the smallest of all nods for Miss Dexter to understand. Sally was to perform next and she really did not want to go out on the floor and be humiliated by the judges, so she had asked Miss Dexter if someone else could take her place. When Miss Dexter went up to Sally and whispered in her ear that she had one of the reserves who would like to take her place, she accepted the suggestion readily. Just for a moment she had forgotten to ask who was to take her place, but when she saw Claire walk out onto the floor her heart gave a leap of joy. What a fool Claire was about to make of herself, was now what Sally was thinking and how grateful Nancy would be when she learned it was she, Sally, who had given up her place to Claire, so Claire could be humiliated.

CHAPTER 49
Claire Can't be Stopped

Sally's team members could hardly believe their eyes when Claire appeared to perform instead of Sally, and walked up to the edge of the mat while looking around. She sensed their pessimism, but it did not bother her. She started her run and halfway across the mat she propelled herself up into the air, performed some remarkable moves and landed on her feet precisely on the edge of the mat at the other corner. It was over so quickly that if you blinked you would have missed it. Apparently the judges must have been sleeping, for they gave Claire just an ordinary mark while her opponent received a much higher one. Later Claire was called to perform on the four inch beam. She lifted herself onto the beam and immediately began her performance which included a backflip with a full twist which made those watching gasp. Again she just got an ordinary mark from the judge. Claire had not made a fool of herself, but rather the judge had. When it was all over the winning school was announced to be the visiting school. Miss Law was delighted, and once the team had changed, they all headed for the bus and drove off. It had been all down to the judges, who for this match just happened to live in the wealthiest part of the town close to Miss Law's school. They knew most of the parents and grandparents of those in Miss Law's team, and they felt they had no choice but to make sure Miss Law's team won, for otherwise they would have been ostracised by the elite of the area. They just did not want to face the ire of their rich friends. so even Claire and her remarkable performances had to be made to look ordinary.

Of course Sally blamed Claire for the defeat, but the rest of the team, except Sally's two friends, were having none of it. The only person gullible enough to swallow the lie would be Nancy which was all that Sally wanted. Several more events took place and then the competition ended and the winner of the league was proclaimed. It turned out to be none other than Miss Law's group of gymnasts and in second place was to be found Miss Dexter's group. Every year the first and second placed clubs had a contest to find which club would be given the honour of gymnastics club of the year. It was to be held in the town's sports hall in a few days time, with the winner of the play-off being presented with the Champions Cup.

Before the event Miss Dexter called a meeting of the gymnastics junior club to discuss the team selection. "After Claire's remarkable performance in the last event, I think Claire should be promoted from being a reserve in the team to actually a position on the team. We shall take a hand vote on that, right now." The vote was taken and all in the club, except Sally and her two friends, voted for Claire's inclusion in the upcoming match.

Claire put up her hand and got permission to speak. "Please Miss," said Claire, "I would never want to replace anyone in the team. After all, it's the final and I'm just a newcomer. The rest of the team has worked so hard throughout the year to get to the final, so everyone in that team deserves to be in the final including the reserves. I of course will be in the audience cheering you on. Sally, who is such an accomplished gymnast, sacrificed her position the last time we met them, allowing me to take her place, so I would never want anyone to do such a noble thing again. I believe our present team can win the event on Saturday. They were much better than the other team and now that there will be three independent judges from another town, I say again we can win, without my help!" Claire was applauded for her speech by everyone in the room including Sally and her friends.

"Well said, Claire!" cried Miss Dexter. "Of course we can win as Claire says. I don't know what I was thinking when I suggested Claire was to be in the team." A cheer went up from all the members of the club and the meeting came to a close.

Well, they did win on Saturday, and they won

handsomely. Claire had watched the event with other spectators in the town hall and they all went to the dressing room to congratulate the team. Claire congratulated every member of the team for their winning performance and shook hands with each one including Sally. She thought she saw a glimmer of a smile on Sally's face as they shook hands. As Claire made her way home she prayed that what had happened today could be the start of a friendship with Sally and her friends.

CHAPTER 50
Claire and Cindy

Claire had longed to meet her friend Cindy ever since returning to the school. However, Cindy was nowhere to be found and even when she asked about Cindy no one would give her an answer. Claire knew that something was wrong and went to see Miss Clark, who was in charge of their year group. She was reluctant to say much about Cindy, but due to Claire's persistence she at last broke the news to Claire. "We think Cindy is dying," Miss Clark told Claire, who was expecting bad news, but not as bad as it turned out to be.

"Can I please visit, Cindy?" Claire asked.

"I'm afraid not," said Miss Clark, in a quiet, sympathetic voice. "Her mother categorically said she wanted no visitors, especially Cindy's friends. It would upset Cindy and upset her friends too." Claire did not argue, thanked Miss Clark and left. Claire would pray every night for her friends, and Cindy was always in her prayers, but now Claire said an emergency prayer as she made her way back to the playground.

Claire was surprised that some days later Miss Clark sent for Claire with news concerning Cindy. "I received a phone call from Cindy's mother just a short time ago saying that Cindy had requested that Claire would visit her. It's left up to you whether you want to go or not."

"May I go right now, Miss?" asked Claire. Miss Clark looked straight into Claire's eyes and saw her desire to meet Cindy was sincere. She felt Claire had the strength of character to deal with the situation, but nevertheless she still hesitated before answering Claire's question before she spoke.

"Yes, you may go, Claire. I will tell your teacher you will be absent from class."

Cindy stayed close to the school so it was not long before Claire was standing at Cindy's front doorstep ringing the bell. The door was opened by Cindy's mother, who looked sad and completely exhausted. She let Claire in but said nothing for there was nothing to say. She went up the stairs and Claire followed. She then went into Cindy's bedroom while Claire waited at the bedroom door. She could hear Cindy's mother's soft voice, but no words from Cindy. After a few minutes Cindy's mother came to the door. "She'll see you now, Claire," she said, as she left the door open for Claire to enter.

Claire found the room to be quite dark for the curtains were partially drawn, but Claire could see just as well in a darkened room as in a bright one. There was a chair which had been purposely placed near the head of the bed and it was there that Claire sat down. "Hello," whispered Claire. Cindy smiled. Claire then heard the bedroom door close leaving the two friends alone in the room, for Cindy had asked her mother that it could be arranged that way.

Claire took hold of her friend's hand and held it gently and was not going to let go unless asked to do so. "I'm so afraid of dying, Claire," whispered Cindy. "You know I have done so many bad things before we became friends. Shall I be punished when I die for all these bad things I did, not only to you Claire, but to lots of others.

"I can see the Holy Spirit has been working in your life Cindy, making you think of salvation. I have long forgiven you Cindy and you helped save my life on the cliff top that day, but if you believe in The Lord Jesus Christ, that He took your punishment on the cross, how can God punish you when He has already punished His Son for your sins?"

"I never thought of that, for that would be silly punishing the two. As you say, God has already punished His Son for the bad things I have done. Could you open the curtains just a little bit more please, Claire, so I can see your face. Claire rose and let the light into the room. "You have told me these things before Claire, and now I believe I won't be going to hell if I die, shall I?"

"No, you shan't, and I won't be going either along with millions around the world who believe that

The Lord Jesus Christ took the punishment they all deserved, but there was something else I used to worry about when I die. Perhaps you are worrying about it too. I still do wrong things and think wrong thoughts, and when God looks at me, He sees I am not perfect and not fit for heaven. Now we know The Lord Jesus Christ led a perfect, sinless life and when we believe on the Lord Jesus Christ, He will clothe us in His perfect righteousness, so when God looks on us He sees us as being righteous, and so we can enter heaven. Cindy, do you believe He took your place on the cross where He took the punishment for your sins, and that The Lord Jesus Christ led a spotless, sinless, righteous life, and His righteousness has been gifted to you. Do you believe that, Cindy?"

"Yes I do, Claire," answered Cindy.

"Well you are saved, and not going to hell for the Lord took your punishment. You can now enter heaven because He has clothed you in His righteousness. When God looks upon you he sees you as sinless for you are clothed in His Son's righteousness. That annoys a lot of people who are proud, and like to think that they can earn heaven by doing good things and giving lots of money away. Of course, once you are saved you just can't help but do good things to help others and tell people of The Lord Jesus Christ." Cindy squeezed Claire's hand.

"Your mother, Cindy, will be getting anxious by

now, so I better go." Claire could see that Cindy was looking tired, but still looked better than when she entered the room which gave Claire hope. Claire took hold of Cindy's other hand and while holding now both her hands said a short prayer. "I shall call again today at lunchtime, if you like, and then tomorrow at the morning interval, if you choose.

"I would like that," said Cindy, as their hands separated. Claire went down stairs where she thanked Cindy's mother and asked if she could call again.

"Well, you might as well know, I don't approve of your visit. However, Cindy wanted it, so I acquiesced to her request, but I think it's best if she now has no more visits.|I don't agree with all your prayers and religious talks you give her, so kindly just stay away from here. She showed Claire to the door and opened it wide for Claire to walk through, for in her mind Claire carried with her a load of baggage. Claire reckoned that Cindy's mother must have been listening in to their conversation. She returned to school and reported back to Miss Clark who was saddened when she heard there were to be no more visits.

"Miss Clark, what exactly is wrong with Cindy?" asked Claire.

"No one knows," answered Miss Clark. "They think it may be something she had eaten."

As for Claire, she believed that it could be spiritual and Cindy was making herself ill as a punishment.

She asked if she could have an extended morning break if needed in the future. Miss Clark agreed to the request saying that she wished Cindy's mother would relent and permit Claire to visit Cindy again. That night Claire prayed that Miss Clark's wish would be granted.

CHAPTER 51
Prayers Answered

Claire's prayers were answered, for next morning Cindy's mother contacted the school with the message that Claire could continue her visits to Cindy. Miss Clark conveyed the good news to Claire. Importunity had been awarded again.

Claire did visit Cindy every day where they would pray together, and every day Claire noticed an improvement in her friend's health. Cindy's mother also noticed the improvement in her daughter's health since the start of Claire's visits. Just for a moment she believed the improvement and Claire's visits were linked, but then she rejected that thought thinking that such an idea was rather ridiculous. No, her daughter's improvement was all due to the skilful nursing she had provided, and that alone.

The time came when it was obvious to all that Cindy was back to full health. One day Claire asked Cindy's mother if Cindy would now be returning to school. "I don't think so," snapped Cindy's mum. "Cindy needs nursing every day and that is one thing the school cannot provide. If it were not for my nursing she would still be lying on her sick bed, so don't you bring up the subject of returning to school every again, Claire. If you do, you will no longer be welcome in this house." Claire felt that for the sake of Cindy's health that Cindy should get back to the normal routine of school life, and urged that Cindy's mum let her go. Needless to say, Claire was then banned from visiting Cindy forthwith.

It was soon noticed by Miss Clark that Claire no longer visited Cindy daily, so one day Miss Clark sent for Claire to find the reason why. Claire told Miss Clark how she had been banned from visiting Cindy, because she had argued that Cindy should be back in school. Miss Clark phoned Cindy's mum insisting on a medical certificate stating just why Cindy was still absent. Well it turned out for the best for Cindy, for the doctor found Cindy in very good health and it was quite safe for her to return to school

That very next morning when Claire was leaving the school bus she noticed Cindy on her own, walking through the school gates and heading off to the school office to announce her return. "I just knew that you could bring that about, Miss Clark," whispered Claire to herself when she saw Cindy enter the building. Claire smiled and thanked God.

Cindy's first class of the day was history, so Cindy lined up out outside the classroom with some of the class who were so happy to see her back. Right on time the teacher opened the classroom door and in filed the class. They all sat down, including Cindy in her usual seat unnoticed by her teacher. He read out the role as usual, and when it came to Cindy's name he was just about to tick the box for absent when the sound of "Present Sir" rang out. The teacher dropped his pen and lifted up his head to find to his amazement Cindy seated at her usual place with a big smile on her face. He took out his handkerchief from his breast pocket and dabbed his eyes as if some dust had just blown into them.

At the morning interval, and before it had started, Miss Clark was having a chat with Cindy in her office, so Claire never saw Cindy again until lunchtime in the canteen. Claire and her group of friends were all seated at their usual table and were about to start their meal when Claire spotted Cindy approaching with her tray. She came right up to the table. "May I join you?" she asked.

It's Cindy!" exclaimed Eleanor, who rose and took Cindy's tray and helped her to sit down. They were all so glad to see Cindy looking so well and sitting beside them.

Rosie felt she just had to pray. She thanked God for Cindy's good health, for Cindy joining them and that they would all become good friends. Also, of course, she thanked God for the food they were about to eat.

CHAPTER 52

The Concert

One day when Claire was helping at the *Vets Vets Vets* surgery, Mrs Willis, who ran the surgery, approached Claire asking for her help. "Our finances are running low Claire and the committee really needs your help."

"To help set up another concert?" asked Claire. Mrs Willis nodded. "I would be delighted to help."

"We were hoping you would say that, Claire. The last time you were the soloist in the Tchaikovsky first piano concerto, it was such an arousing success we were wondering if you would be the soloist again in some other concerto?"

"I enjoyed playing here and would jump at the chance to do it all over again. Thank you so much Mrs Willis for picking me as your soloist."

Mrs Willis then spent the next few days contacting the local amateur youth orchestra, the very orchestra that Claire had performed with before. Unfortunately, they flatly turned down the idea of another piano concerto with Claire. They gave no reason, but a friend of Mrs Willis, whose son was in the local youth orchestra, spilt the beans. It turned out to be envy, for the last time Claire had received all the praise, but the orchestra was just ignored. No, they never wanted to play along with Claire ever again, and they were quite adamant about it. Mrs Willis thanked her friend and said they would try something else to help the charity.

When Claire heard the explanation from Mrs Willis she just sighed and gave a cynical smile. "What do you think we can do?" asked Claire.

"They won't let us use the Town Hall if we don't have the youth orchestra," said Mrs Willis. "We shall just have to use the school hall and we will be lucky if we fill that. We really do need to raise some money to help the animals."

Claire could see that Mrs Willis was very upset. "I think the youth orchestra just think about themselves and don't care at all about animals," said Claire.

"Don't worry Claire, you and I may be able to persuade the school orchestra to partake in the Tchaikovsky first piano concerto with you playing the piano, Claire," said Mrs Willis, thinking that might be the answer to the problem. What do you think Claire?"

"You never know. I do wonder," said Claire, with a friendly smile. "They might just."

Mrs Willis was taken by surprise by Claire's enthusiasm, and a faint smile appeared on her lips. "You're right Claire, they might just. If anyone can persuade them to take part it will be you, Claire." Mrs Willis was spot on for Claire actually persuaded Mr East, a retired gentleman, who was the volunteer conductor of the school orchestra, and Miss Beach, the head of music at the school who ran the Senior and Junior choirs to meet Miss Willis at the vets on Saturday morning.

Miss Beach, a pet owner, wanted the meeting to be fruitful. She knew Mr East had a pet dog called Rusty, and she wanted him to see the good work done by *Vets Vets Vets,* so the meeting had been arranged to be at the surgery. On Saturday morning the meeting took place in Mrs Willis' office. Miss Beach said her choirs were always ready to sing in public at the school hall and their parents were always keen to attend. Mr East had heard of Claire but had never seen her perform. He just did not know if the school orchestra and Claire were experienced enough to carry it off.

"What experience have you had at playing with an orchestra?" he asked Claire.

"Claire has played the Tchaikovsky first piano concerto under the baton of Sir Robert Buchanan," said Mrs Willis, knowing that Claire might just be too modest to tell. He had not known that having been away on a cruise when it occurred.

"Well, I think we should play the Tchaikovsky first, for you must be already proficient in playing it. All we need now is to get the School Orchestra up to standard and we can go ahead with the

Tchaikovsky first," said Mr East, as he glanced at his watch. "It's only nine thirty and the orchestra meets every Saturday morning at ten in the school. Why not come to our rehearsal, Mrs Willis, and tell them all about your charity and your plans for the concerto. If you bring Claire too in your own car, then you could be back here by half ten."

So they all did go to the rehearsal where Mrs Willis made a great speech about her animal charity and had the whole orchestra wanting to help. Mr East and Miss Beach learned a lot about the charity and at the end of Mrs Willis' speech was very enthusiastic about helping. From the music store room in the school Mr East collected the music scores that were needed and handed them out so rehearsals could start that very day.

On Monday morning Mrs Willis went to visit the headteacher who agreed to host the concert as part of their charity work with the local community. Soon the orchestra was ready to play in public. It was to take place in the school hall on a Saturday morning, with the school orchestra and the school choirs.

CHAPTER 53
The Concert

The day for the concerto with Claire being the soloist soon arrived. The school orchestra had spent many hours rehearsing and now at last Mr East was satisfied with their performance. Claire just wanted to be treated like anyone else in the orchestra for she could see that envy and resentment could result if she was the star of the show. The concert began with the Senior choir singing, *All Things Bright and Beautiful* This was followed by them singing some traditional folk songs. After that it was the junior choir's turn to entertain the audience. The curtain then fell just for a moment and then rose again.

There was no interval just in case some of the audience slipped away having only come to see their children sing. The time had now come when the orchestra had to take up their positions on the stage. The whole orchestra, including Claire, in white shirt and school tie, walked on to the stage and took up their places. Claire sat down at the piano which was at the front of the stage, but not in the middle as was the custom. The orchestra tuned up and the applause broke out in the hall as Mr East appeared on stage from a side door, walked over to the podium and took up his position. When he saw all were ready he raised his baton and the orchestra began to play followed by Claire. The young orchestra performed magnificently despite one or two hiccups on the way, but not one person in the audience noticed for they were there to enjoy themselves and admire their children. It was indeed a great success and when it came to an end, never in the history of the hall had there been such applause and cheers.

When calm had returned Mrs Willis came on stage and thanked them all for supporting her charity, for all profit made was to be given to *Vets Vets Vets.* Mrs Willis thanked all who had helped to set up the concert, but knew not to mention Claire's name. The headteacher then gave a short speech.

The show had ended and now it was time for those taking part to meet with friends and relatives. Claire sought out Mr East and congratulated him on his great success. "I don't know how you managed to keep the orchestra all playing as one. You really are an amazing conductor, Mr East."

"Why, thank you Claire. "Well I had a great solo pianist in the orchestra who did most of the work keeping them all playing together."

"Thank you Mr East, but the pianist still thinks it was you who held them all together. It was the most thrilling rendering I have ever witnessed. The way we all ended as a group was so awesome. I'm sure the members of the orchestra will never forget that moment." Claire then spotted the headteacher approaching, no doubt to congratulate Mr East, so Claire slipped away to leave them alone. Mrs Willis noticed Claire and came over to speak.

"Where are all your friends, Claire?" asked Mrs Willis when she saw Claire along with Cindy.

"I asked them not to come," replied Claire, to the astonishment of Mrs Willis. "I knew they would not like to have seen me delegated to a position at the side of the stage and not walk on and off the stage followed by the conductor. The concerto was about us making money to help sick and wounded animals, nothing to do with me."

The hall began to empty. Claire left with Cindy who had sung in the Junior choir. Her mother met up with them and invited Claire to lunch at their home. Claire accepted the invitation after contacting her mum. Soon they were seated round the kitchen table with Cindy's mother saying grace. The prayer may have ended but not the tears from Claire's eyes, that had begun at the start of the prayer.

They did have a very nice launch which Cindy and her mum had prepared beforehand. When it was time to leave Claire thanked them and left to walk home alone, which would take her about an hour. As she walked she thought of Cindy and her amazing recovery. She just could not hold back and sang several hymns praising God for there was no one else around. She heard the high pinched song of a little bird that seemed to accompany her in her praise. She looked up and there among the branches of a tree she spotted a little robin red breast. She saluted the little bird as a marvel of God's creation.

CHAPTER 54
Claire is Asked to Help

One Sunday, after the morning church service, Mr Aldwyn once again drove the Gospel Bus with the gospeltears to the housing estate where they were going to hold their gospel service. As Claire was helping to get everything ready for the meeting, which was timed to start in half an hour, a young lady called Polly arrived. She was a regular at the Gospel Bus meetings and would bring children along with her to hear the gospel. Polly asked Claire if she could have a private word with her and her sister after the gospel meeting had finished. She lived close by so Claire agreed, but she needed Mrs Flowers' permission. Mrs Flowers agreed as long as Jennifer accompanied her. Claire thought that was a good idea.

So Claire and Jennifer went to Polly's home after the service where they met her sister Alison. Polly then asked Claire if she could help them. "My elder sister, Alison, and I have a friend Judith, who is in trouble," she told them.

"Her mother was killed in a car accident a

few months back and her father now looks after Judith," said Alison. "Her father wants her to marry a rich old man, but Judith does not want to marry him."

"How can we help her?" asked Claire.

"I have still more to tell you," said Alison, and then continued her narrative. "Judith and I work for the same company and I haven't seen Judith or heard from her for three days now. I think she is a prisoner in her own bedroom and her father won't let her out until she agrees to the marriage." Here Alison stopped talking and looked at Claire in desperation hoping she had the solution to the problem. "What am I going to do?" she cried out, as she bent her head and held it in her hand as she started to weep.

Her younger sister, who was sitting next to her on the settee, moved closer and placed a comforting arm around her. "My friends will help us," she told her sister.

"But they are just young girls against a grown up man. "Why did
you bring them. You have just made things worse, Polly?"

"I was there when Claire saved a boy's life. If anyone can rescue Alison it's Claire and Jennifer."

Claire, who was sitting directly opposite the two sisters was now feeling slightly embarrassed, so Claire now felt obliged to speak. "I'll do my very best, but I shall need your help. Do you want me to help you?" asked Claire, coming right to the point.

Alison looked up and gazed at Claire through her tears. "I have been very rude," she said, "and yes, I want you to help." Claire asked her several questions about the house and the father's habits

Claire and Jennifer then went back to the Gospel Bus where Mrs Flowers had been waiting for them. They were accompanied by Polly and Alison who were introduced to Mrs Flowers. "We are going back to the church now," said Mrs Flowers, "where we are going to have our lunch and then get ready for Sunday School at three o'clock. Would both of you like to join us for lunch, for I can run you back home after lunch in my car?" The both accepted Mrs Flowers' invitation.

After lunch Mrs Flowers, Claire and Jennifer along with their guests went into a private room to find out what exactly was going on. Polly told Mrs Flowers all about Judith. "We are going to rescue her, but we will need a place to hide her," said Claire, with her pleading eyes fixed on Mrs Flowers.

Mrs Flowers smiled. "Very well, Claire, she can stay in my house." They all thanked Mrs Flowers for her generosity. I am now going to let Claire conduct proceedings, so you will now be in charge, Claire."

"Thank you, Mrs Flowers, so I shall start with Polly. Please tell us all you know about Judith's father and what you think he will be doing tomorrow at lunch time?"

"He does not have a job just now," said Polly. "At

noon he goes to the fast food restaurant and then to the pub. He returns home at two. That is what I have seen him do when the college is on holiday."

"Would you say he was a lazy man?"

"He is very lazy," said Polly.

"What do you say, Alison?" asked Claire.

"I concur."

"That is all I need to know," said Claire.

Claire then phoned her friend Brice and asked if he could supply her with a delivery van like those used to deliver parcels for people ordering online. She also asked if he could supply several empty cardboard boxes and four hi vis yellow jackets, two for younger and two for older persons. He was only too happy to help Claire and assured her a van would be there on Mrs Flowers' driveway before eleven o'clock tomorrow morning.

"We shall rescue Judith tomorrow at lunch time," Claire stated emphatically. "We are not going to let Judith suffer a second longer than necessary."

"I'm afraid I can't manage to be there tomorrow," said Alison regrettably. "In no way would my boss give me the time off."

"It's alright Alison, don't worry," said Claire sympathetically.

"I can manage," said Polly quickly. "It will be during our lunch time at the college."

"Mrs Flowers will first pick up Jennifer and myself in the van near the school at the start of our lunch break, then Polly near her college. Claire next went on to tell each of them what role they would play tomorrow in her plan to save Judith.

Now Claire felt it was important to stay anonymous for their own safety and well being. She did not want Judith's father finding out who they were and seeking revenge on them. "He seems a rather vindictive man. Judith must never know who rescued her, except of course for Polly," said Claire to them. "Tonight I want you all to pray that by lunchtime tomorrow, Judith will be safe and secure and will be having lunch in Mrs Flowers' kitchen."

CHAPTER 55
The Rescue

The next day Brice was true to his word and delivered the van in Mrs Flowers' driveway. At lunch time Mrs Flowers picked up Claire, Jennifer and Polly as had been arranged in the van. Claire and Polly then disguised themselves as a delivery crew, and Jennifer changed from her school uniform into her everyday clothes.

A short time later the van pulled up close to the fast food restaurant where Judith's father was known to hang out. Jennifer went into the restaurant and came out eating a burger. That was the signal that meant Judith's father was in there. Judith then had to hang about eating her burger and to let them know if he left the restaurant. Mrs Flowers drove the short distance to Judith's house and parked outside it.

Claire sprang out the van followed by Polly. They looked like delivery men carrying parcels. When she reached the front door, Claire with her bunch of skeleton keys, managed to open it quite easily. They both ran up the stairs to Judith's room which was at the back of the house. The key to Judith's room was in the door, so Claire was right, the man was too lazy to hide the key and just left it in the lock

"Who's there?" came the terrified voice of Judith from within the bedroom. "It's Polly, come to set you free." Claire turned the key and slowly opened the door.

Polly ran up to Judith with outstretched arms and gave her the biggest hug she had ever received from a friend.

"We must leave now," said Claire, who was calm and collective. "I have brought this big bag if there is anything you want to take with you, Judith."

"Just the photos in the frames." Claire helped her gather up the photos and put them in the bag.

"You better go now," said Claire. "I'll put the room back exactly as it was. All you have to do is crush the empty boxes we brought and put them back in the van. Be careful going down stairs." Claire went over to the bedroom window that overlooked the back garden and using one of the skeleton keys unlocked it then opened it slightly. Anyone seeing the window open and wondering how Judith managed to escape would assume she left through the window. Polly and Judith had now left the house and were heading for the van. They were soon followed by Claire who had locked the bedroom door then the front door of the house.

"How long were we?" asked Polly, when they had closed the sliding door of the van.

"Just about ninety seconds, but it seemed like

half an hour to me sitting here waiting," said Mrs Flowers. As soon as Claire was back in the van they moved off as if they were looking for the next house to deliver to. When they were well away from the scene of the crime, for it was a crime to lock up Judith, Claire then phoned Jennifer and told her the good news and they were coming to pick her up as there was now no need to keep an eye on Judith's father. Soon Polly was back at the college having her lunch in the canteen while Jennifer and Claire were in the school canteen having lunch with their friends. As for Mrs Flowers, well Mrs Flowers was back home with the van parked in her driveway. She contacted Claire, who then contacted Brice and thanked him, who came and collected the van.

As for Judith, well after having a shower to help wash away the memory of her imprisonment, she could be found seated at Mrs Flowers' kitchen table, having the best meal she ever had in a long time.

CHAPTER 56
Claire's Homeward Journey

One Saturday a few weeks later, Cindy invited Claire to launch on Saturday at her house. That morning Claire took Big Dog and Mitzy for a walk up to see her friends Eleanor and Rosie at their farms. After breakfast she fed Big Hen and Wee Gem then visited the local vets charity to help for an hour. Next she visited her friend Mrs Carmichael and helped her in her cottage and on her smallholding. When the time drew near to Cindy's invitation for lunch she caught a bus from outside the golf course next to Mrs Carmichael's field. Claire was soon to be found knocking at Cindy's door. After her meal she decided to walk home rather than catch the bus, opting to take the shortcut through the city park. Her favourite feature of the park was the boating pond where enthusiastic model makers brought their boats to sail.

There was a path all the way round the pond and a gentle grassy slope down to the water. As Claire watched the people sailing their boats it was then she spotted a small boy, with a young lady looking after him, at a quiet part of the pond. The boy, who was too young to attend school, was sailing a little wooden boat modelled on the Queen Mary. He would, with the help of the young lady, push the boat out into the pond and move it about with a long walking stick, then pull it back in with the string attached to it. Claire stood and watched them from afar enjoying the tranquillity of the park.

However, that was all to change in the twinkling of an eye. Two youths had swaggered up to the young lady with the small boy and were now standing watching them with intent. Claire sensed they were up to no good, so she hid behind a rhododendron bush and in less than one minute reappeared disguised as a boy, a disguise she had used before with success. The boy was wearing a cap and a large pair of spectacles, so as to hide as much of Claire's face as possible. There was no backpack, for Claire had hidden it behind the rhododendron bush.

The two youths were now picking up stones and small rocks and started throwing them at the boy's boat. As they kept missing their target they became more and more frustrated and started to pick up larger objects to throw. The young lady looking after the boy was becoming anxious for their safety and told the two youths to stop throwing things at the boat. "Just who are you, telling *me* what to do?" called out the youth, with the tattoos on his bare arms as he advanced towards the young lady. Claire, in her disguise, now felt it was time to intervene and ran right up to the youth blocking his path.

"Get out my way," he yelled, as he stretched out his hand to push Claire aside. Claire easily grabbed hold of his tattooed arm and pulled him forward in such a way that when she let go he went tumbling into the shallow part of the pond. Claire just stood there and looked around waiting to see what he would do next. The young lady and the boy had fled with the boat and the walking stick. The other youth just stood staring in front of himself unable to take in what had just happened. The people who were there to sail their boats had stopped what they were doing and had been watching what was happening. Some of them were using their phones to record the event.

The tattooed youth, soaked and dripping water, struggled to his feet and walked up the slope to his partner. On his way up the slope he bent down and took out a knife that he had strapped to the bottom of his leg. He held it in his hand and brandished it in the air as he spat out deadly threats to Claire, who was still standing close to the edge of the pond."Don't be stupid. Put the knife away," screamed his partner. He just ignored his partner and glared at him. His partner had had enough, for he didn't want to be involved in the murder of a child. That did not daunt the tattooed youth who seemed to grow even angrier. He rushed at Claire flashing the blade here, there and everywhere, while Claire stood, watched and then acted. Swish swish swish, was all she heard as the blade cut through the air

She wasn't going to turn her back on anyone wielding a knife, so she started to run up the slope towards him, not right into his face, but to the side of him. She passed him easily because just for a moment he appeared to be disorientated. Claire had done the exact opposite of what he had been expecting to happen. When he had regained his senses it was too late for him, for Claire had stopped running and had turned round and was now behind him. She gave his back a hefty push so he stumbled down the slope and once again landed in the water. This time he did not get to his feet but just sat there in the shallow water with his head in his hands.

Claire went down to the side of the pond and offered him her hand to pull him up and out of the water. He saw this as his only chance to redeem himself. He took hold of her hand, but instead of letting Claire pull him out of the water he tried to pull her into the pond. All his scheming was in vain for Claire gave him such a yank that he landed on his stomach on the grassy slope around the pond, where he lay and just groaned and wept.

None of those watching what had just happened had come to the boy's aid, but they had recorded it all on their phones. Claire was therefore glad that she had disguised herself as the boy, for it would soon all be on social media and something surely would be done about it. Claire then quickly left the boating pond and went to her rhododendron bush and emerged a short time later as Claire with her backpack on. As she walked out through the gates of the city park she could hear the sound of a police serine. "Someone must have phoned the police. Oh, I am so glad I disguised myself." She then prayed and thanked God for His help and asked Him to look after the young lady with the small boy who must have had a very harrowing experience.

Claire had had a very eventful day and was looking forward to getting home and being with her mum and friends once again. As she walked she thanked God once more for Cindy's recovery and pondered what the future would bring. Well, that is another story altogether.